Have You Seen CindySleigh?

HAVE YOU SEEN CINDYSLEIGH?

& OTHER STORIES

DIANE STIGLICH

POETS WEAR PRADA • Hoboken, New Jersey

Have You Seen CindySleigh?

Poets Wear Prada
533 Bloomfield Street, Second Floor
Hoboken, New Jersey 07030
http://pwpbooks.blogspot.com

First North American Publication 2016
First Mass Market Paperback Edition 2016

ISBN-13: 978-0997981117
ISBN-10: 0997981113

Library of Congress Control Number: 2016955277

Printed in the U.S.A.

Front Cover Image: Diane Stiglich
Author Photo: Craig Wallace Dale

For Jim Supplee

Table of Contents

HAVE YOU SEEN CINDYSLEIGH?

HAVE YOU SEEN CINDYSLEIGH?

The birds wake up CindySleigh, with the early sun. She feels glad to get up before the loud construction sounds have started across the street. The new massive rectangles keep appearing. She can still smell the dampness of the Hudson River before the endless fugue of noise begins. She closes her eyes, but no more sleep is there. All she can see is the bulky manila hemp of a noose hanging before her. The sturdy chair, made of recycled wood, would give her a steady climb so she would not fall before killing herself. This detail somehow seems important. Cindy has been waking up and having this vision for six months, but as her Uncle Fred used to say, "You don't have to kill yourself. Death meets everyone. You just have to be patient. Death will come." So, she slowly reconsiders.

Cindy does not really want to put a noose around her neck; she just cannot stay in this particular place on this earth anymore. Perhaps another place would do. "I do have legs that work, a truck that works, and three credit cards Father Michael won't cancel because he worships me. I will escape. I will run away."

Cindy loves to run. It always makes her feel free. Although this run is for real, Cindy does what she always does when she runs: check the weather. If she does not check the weather, how will she know which way to go?

Teterboro, 90 ... Newark, 92 ... winds from the west at twenty miles an hour. With a gust of decision, Cindy grabs her precious Tarot cards. Lately she has drawn only the Two of Swords — its seated white-robed figure, blindfolded, at an impasse, arms crossed at the elbows, holding two swords poised to cut the unseen air. Cindy checks her pure white crew cut and then throws on her white Wranglers and a crisp, white long-sleeved shirt over her Wednesday pink silk boy shorts and matching bra. Running shoes are essential for running away. Cindy's silver iPod, filled with the same two hundred songs housed for over a year, will last indefinitely for this family of one. All this preparation to avoid Father Michael and D.C. — more about that later.

Cindy looks into the mirror, her reflection confirming she is in essential form. She slides on her white-framed shades, grabs her purse and three sets of keys (a countermeasure taken due to her ability to easily lose things), and bounds out of the apartment. Feeling more free than God she runs to her beloved black Chevy pickup, throws it into first gear, and heads due west on Route 80 quickly accelerating to 75 miles per hour. Cindy has never gotten a ticket. Maybe the cop would prove to be, y'know, interesting, if she gets caught.

The cliffs of the Delaware Water Gap seem far off, as a bottle of champagne appears next to her in the passenger seat. Cindy pulls over under the guidance of a Scenic

View Here sign — as if the state has to tell you where to see beauty. A light scream leaps from her throat as the bottle pops open. She pours some champagne onto the ground in thanks to the muse that sent it. Ah, the misty bubbles of which dreams are made. Her iPod perfectly times the musical overlay of the moment: "My Faith is Gone." Licking her index finger and waving it in the air, she senses the wind is blowing strongly from the west. Forward then, into the wind.

Entering Pennsylvania definitely lifts her mood, along with the champagne. Here, in the early morning glow, the naked trees are lavender and the roads are pink. "Grass is greener on the other side." The tune matches her mood. Cindy pushes the pedal to the floor, but the damn truck refuses to match her speed. Fast is never fast enough when you need to get away. There are always those lines in the airport, the computer freezing, the bad connection on the cell phone — not that Cindy bothered with anything electronic. "They sap your life's spirit," she would say. "The muses never come while *Jeopardy* blares from the television." She enjoys the silence of the morning, filling it with music, keeping time with the day, while her iPod blares on.

Ah! He appears behind her on his white motorcycle, red lights flashing, provocatively, to pull her over — her penalty for rushing through life. The gods request patience. Running away never really works because the earth is ultimately round, and wherever you go, you are still there. They roll to a stop together. He is exactly Cindy's size. Five foot nine inches tall, slight but strongly built. He takes off his hat, revealing a matching crew cut. "What's your hurry, cowgirl?"

Cindy looks up as silent tears run down her face. "I am tired of useless desires," the iPod howls; however, no words come out of her mouth. She closes the truck door and walks into the woods, leaving behind her iPod. Deer spring ahead of her, showing their white tails and glancing back to make sure she follows. "There he was," Cindy thinks as she keeps following the deer, "a man in a uniform, and all I could do was walk away."

Cindy tilts her head, curious about the crunch of fallen leaves steadily growing louder behind her. Lo and behold, as he catches up to her, the deer stop, and a bottle of champagne appears. "Well, alrighty then. I must need to stop here," Cindy whispers to herself. Just to make sure, she licks her finger and waves it above her head. No wind.

The deer settle in, eating grass near a mist-shrouded

pond. The purr of the distant iPod fades out in the middle of "too close for comfort now." The silence is deafening. She stiffly marches with her fists clenched, shouting, "Bring me the magic, bring me the magic." What worked for Prospero does not work for Cindy; she gives up and sits down.

Cindy has not noticed the young buck that has curled up behind her back so she can rest. She has not noticed the mist that has steadily increased, creating fog. There always has been a thick fog in front of CindySleigh. Before her appears the officer complete with mirrored aviator glasses. She offers him her white-framed shades; he accepts, and they switch sunglasses. Cindy notices he does not have a special face. Like Cindy's it is regular with regular features, not unhandsome but like he could be anybody. There is blankness in his eyes: the deer have it, Cindy has it, and Officer Eric has it. Eyes that do not let anybody in, that stop, in a moment, as the spirit evacuates the body. When this happens, it does not matter if you are hurt. When pain comes, it is of no consequence, for the spirit has already retreated so deeply that it will never be found, not even by another soul.

The lack of music sets her back into a panic. To avoid eye contact, Cindy puts on the aviator glasses and feels an inch of comfort. Eric sits down and scans Cindy, starting with her baby-chick of a crew cut. Avoiding the sun's glint off her mirrored shades, he pauses at the small rivulets tracing her flushed cheeks, then takes in a strong female frame — seemingly incongruous — dressed in white. The pronounced veins on her hands match his from ten-too-many push-ups — his sweat in preparation for his job and life. Cindy murmurs nonsense to the young buck who somehow has become hers, and it begins to lick her hand.

Cindy shifts gears in her mind, from first to fifth with speed. "Oh hello, have some champagne, how rude of me." Opening the bottle, she lets out a shriek — a little joy, a little pain, the mix of escape. Eric sits before her. He accepts a cup, and together they sip slowly, their eyes never meeting, hidden behind sunglasses. Cindy, playing the good hostess, offers to read Eric his Tarot cards. She pulls a pink bag out of her white purse and slowly unwraps them. (A ritual taught to her by Marc, her muse.) She shuffles the cards, making crisp cardboard sounds that become a soft staccato in the stillness of the fog.

Eric's first card turned is the Knight of Cups. Cindy sighs to herself — no man of action here. Then she sees another overflowing cup of emotions. The blindfolded figure of the Two of Swords is disappearing from each card Cindy lays down. Eric is crowned by the King of Swords. His emotions battle. Beneath him is the Fool. "My friend in folly," Cindy chuckles to herself as she considers his cards. So he begins his journey as the Fool, then surrounds himself with battle. His emotions turn up the Page of Cups.

"Only the beginning," she tells him. "The outcome is the young naked boy, the Sun." She gathers up her cards. Upon touching her hands, the blindfolded figure, a young woman bearing crossed swords, reappears on each card. Cindy breathes in and out, slowly. "Well, for some, patterns come and go," she continues, "and all I can say is, that is not the case for you. Your pattern is set. You love men so much it is killing you. Let's trick the wheel of fate."

Cindy stands up and begins to undress. By the time she is down to her pink Wednesday boy shorts and Eric is only left with his plaid boxers, they do what they must: exchange piles of clothes. As Cindy slips on the boxers and Eric experiences the feel of silk against his skin, they look up at each other and smile. The unspoken world of secrets exchanged, a place exposing ultimate pleasure. Suddenly, Cindy is obsessed with putting on his uniform as quickly as possible, her heart racing. In contrast to her typical pulse of sixty, this means Cindy might actually just be feeling alive. Neither looks up again until the last buttons are buttoned, and Cindy admires how good he looks in white Wranglers. Cindy is sure she died and went to heaven as she looks down at her state trooper's uniform. A ripple of nerves charges through her like a wave. She comments, "Don't worry, Eric, I have always been a homosexual man in a woman's body. You are safe with me, and I'll attract all the men you need like bees to honey. Not just any men —

narcissistic, smart, tight-bodied, strong, focused men so you can be free, yet never bored."

With that pronouncement, she digs a hole and empties the champagne into it. All the deer come to drink. Eric and Cindy do not hold hands as they walk side by side. Backlit by sunlight, their silhouettes seem charged by their exchange. Eric, gingerly, removes his cell phone from the pocket of the uniform Cindy now wears. He dials the weather. West winds at fifty miles an hour. Cindy grabs his cell and throws it as far as she can into the woods. "I hate those damned cell phones," she declares. Sauntering to the motorcycle, Eric tosses her the keys. Cindy, for the first time in months, smiles from ear to ear. She misses the catch. She is clumsy as hell.

Swooping up the keys, Cindy straddles the bike, Eric straddling behind her. Their close bodies smell woodsy, like young animals. She kicks back the stand, turns the key, and roars west with the pink roads and yellow lines whipping beneath her ...

Actually, Cindy has no idea how to drive a motorcycle. Starting out, she hits the brakes instead of the gas and wipes out on the side of the road. Cindy lets Eric drive, telling herself that hugging a great body from behind is even better than driving.

The sound of the wind rushes past her ears like a giant conch mimicking the sea, helping make up for the lost stream of songs that has kept Cindy going.

AS THE SUN sets, they pull into the state police barracks. A police station filled with only seriously macho men:

"Hey guys, how ya doin'?" Cindy assertively asks as she strides forward in uniform. She introduces Eric as "Cindy, my twin. She's stopping by to take a look at how it's done down here at the station."

A few catcalls make Eric blush, much to the satisfaction of his fellow officers.

"You guys don't mind if we bunk together tonight, incest being acceptable and all," Cindy jests in her lowest voice.

"No, no have a ball. Just let us know if he can't keep up with you, sweetie," a police officer cracks.

Eric shoves Cindy in the direction of his room. The door slams behind them, and they both sigh in relief. Cindy pours sweat, her heart pounds. She immediately drops to the floor and does ten push-ups, jumping up with a much clearer head. (This is one of the many skills taught to her by her teacher Sir.)

Eric pulls her head back by yanking down the collar of her uniform. He holds her head with his other hand and French-kisses Cindy until his tongue reaches her toes. Cindy, tingling, extends the fingers of both hands fully, experiencing euphoria and a serious lack of air.

Released, she slumps to the floor and announces, "You totally dismantle me." Ten more push-ups, followed by a bear hug where each is equally strong, squeezing the air out of the other's lungs. "Damn this is good," Cindy manages on an exhale.

They break apart and move to separate sides of the room, pacing back and forth like caged tigers. They look at each other, trying to figure out what to do. Their sexual volley took root, each knowing there could be no real culmination. Their inner desires are askew; their sexual identities have melded together yet remain totally separate.

Cindy remembers a lyric from her lost iPod, "Loving someone too much like yourself is like kissing a mirror. If you love someone who doesn't get you, you will hate yourself in the morning." Cindy cannot figure out which situation this is, then decides it's sad. Eric senses her sadness and walks over to her. He cradles her head in his hands. They stand this way for many minutes without speaking. Then Eric and Cindy sit down next to each other on the bunk bed. They stare straight ahead at the blank wall eight feet in front of them.

As Cindy stares, time takes a brief pause. She watches her young self in a black-and-white film.

* * *

IT ALL BEGAN as a romantic fantasy, as all love does. Cindy met Father Michael when she was just fifteen. He wasn't a priest then — just a mindful Catholic. They spent two wonderful holiday weeks ice skating every day on local creeks with their friends.

Their first date was Christmas Eve midnight mass. Cindy didn't eat all day, and when the priest swung the incense through the aisles, she promptly passed out. She remembers so clearly opening her eyes, seeing Michael's kind face, him saying, "Are you all right? Do you need to leave?" Cindy decided at that moment to marry this man. Cindy is like this, pragmatic and impulsive, making decisions on whim then living in commitment.

Many years passed. They formed a union based on unspoken things. Michael was all verbs and logic. Cindy was all adverbs and chaos.

Later on, when logic became litany, Michael became Father Michael, the part-time priest, keeping all of the church's files in order: day, date, and time. He, God forgive him, could never give up Cindy. There was something, an energy, he needed. He did not understand her; he often was frightened of her. Father Michael kept her in check, loving her too much.

A part-time priest suited Cindy, leaving her free to draw and dream, plant gardens, and read. A inherent wanderer, she'd always go as far as her pink city bicycle would take her.

She is about thirty at this point in time.

When Father Michael would come home from his weekend stint at St. Vincent's, as he'd walked in the door, Cindy would cross herself and say, "Bless me, Father, for I have sinned." She would confess all her fears, indiscretions, and desires. He had a special interest in desires, and they would indulge them all, like the children they were at heart. It was a time of bounty.

Out of the black — it couldn't be blue — D.C. appeared, a six-year-old demon child. Cindy and Father Michael could not have a child, and Cindy could not live without one. "I'll take him," she said, without pausing to breathe.

Father Michael, knowing her impetuousness, cautioned, "Wait, wait, wait. Think, think, think." But Cindy closed her mind to his warnings, and in that moment her slide into hell began. It was a slow slide, a daily rejection of all the love Cindy had to offer. "You can't make me," said the demon child, until rejection became a living wall. There are no words to describe a violation so foreign to Cindy. She only knew that this child, she so wanted to love and save, would reject her, hate her, and torture her. Father Michael, so lost in his litany, never saw, then or now, the lacerations etched into her very marrow by the demon child.

THE WALL WENT blank.

* * *

ATTRACTION WITHOUT FULFILLMENT doesn't last very

long. Cindy puts her hands under Eric's chin and kissed the long kiss of not forever, the long kiss of you won't remember me tomorrow because one face is a thousand faces in a thousand moments. They gently undress each other, each tenderly running hands over the other, touching every part, especially the parts we often forget. The beautiful inside of an elbow or kneecap. Eyelids are a must. A light kiss behind the ear where Eric's hair tastes of the salt of the sea. The next kisses, deep and throaty, are full of goodbyes. All the goodbyes of a lifetime. Standing opposite each other, they re-dress in their "original" clothes (if you could call them that).

Cindy walks out of the door into the night. She pulls some change out of her white purse and calls for the weather from a payphone. Her iPod appears, attached to the receiver. Somebody sings, "I don't have a ghost of a chance with you."

Pittsburgh, sixty-three ... Harrisburg, fifty-nine ... winds from the south at five miles an hour. A good walking speed, Cindy thought. All white in the night, walking down any random road in Pennsylvania. There aren't really that many people once you leave the city. With comfort from her iPod, the night takes on a serenity that only comes just this side of madness. "I'm okay," CindySleigh reminds herself, but she really is afraid.

Cars move past her at lightning speed. Her pace keeps time with the world, and she is good with that. "There's solace for the lonely," the iPod croons. At some point, when sleep seemed inevitable, CindySleigh spies grass — deep-green grass. The color is so saturated and bright; it glows behind the stark black trees. She puts her index finger in her mouth and then holds it stretched high above her head. No wind. Cindy walks over and lies down spread-eagle in this grass, looking up at the indigo sky. She pulls as much of the grass as she can with her hands and her teeth to use as a blanket. Cindy feels full of the taste and the smell of the green. Sleep has found her.

WHEN SHE WAKES, Cindy is immediately aware that something is wrong in the forest. She sniffs and smells the blood of the hunter, Actaeon, out and about, clumsy in his movements. Still covered by green, she remains quiet, waiting for the right second, breathing calmly as Sir has taught her. Actaeon is bearded, big, and broad, but she has been taught that size is only a matter of the mind. This man has no heart, and the deer are in danger. Keeping silent, she slowly rearranges her body to move into action.

Actaeon sees a deer which does not see him and raises his rifle. The next moments are full of contradictory information involving flying grass, a spiraling Cindy round-kicking the hunter in the stomach, gunfire loudly reverberating for miles, and the deer leaping freely away.

The curly-bearded hunter's hat comes off. He falls down, swearing the entire way. Cindy stands back, centered, ready to move again if necessary. The deer of Diana are under her protection. If she can't get her own life up off its ass, the least she can do is to keep the deer safe.

The woods are a sacred place. CindySleigh has been living most of her adult life as a child, so she has the sacredness of the forest carved into her heart of stone. She takes off her white-framed sunglasses and notices small horns on the head of the swearing hunter. He leaps up as easily as the deer. When he sheds his camouflage pants, she can clearly see his goat-like hairy legs and cloven hooves — among other things. He stomps in fury, damning this earthling for ruining tonight's bacchanalia. Cindy waits for him to stop his earth-shaking dance and listens to his breathing until it begins to calm. "These are the deer of Diana. I may have just saved your life, sir," she boldly says.

"Damn you, girl. I am Pan, and now there will be no meat for the feast tonight. There will be many a nymph waiting to transform your life into misery," he threatens.

"Nothing new," Cindy retorts with ease. "You should be a vegetarian anyway, being the rustic god of nature and all," she adds.

"All of nature turns in and eats itself 'round in a circle, stupid child," he fires back. "Y'know, predator-prey. Nature is cruel," he adds impatiently.

"Well I don't care if you are a god. I'm glad I saved that deer, and nature is not allowed to be cruel when it enters the parameters of my world." Cindy's crew cut bristles with her words. Five or six fawns and goats begin to appear and wander around Cindy, eating the grass she wore as a blanket last night. "Look, Pan, I'm just passing through. Good luck with your party." Cindy turns to leave.

"No, no, no, you must stay. You have to stay," he demands.

"I'm not in much of a party mood, unless Russian roulette is part of your game plan," Cindy replies. Pan eyes her with his gold-flecked goat eyes, their centers split by black vertical slits. A brown leather flask appears, and he offers her a swig. "Well, it's really not my usual, but what the hell," Cindy mutters as she begins to drink. Twenty minutes later, he seems not nearly so gruff. Cindy still keeps a bit of distance though, because she doesn't want to wind up like Echo, repeating throughout eternity. A god isn't somebody to be trifled with.

The sun casts its extravaganza before it deserts this side of earth for the day. Her eyes feel heavy, and she hears the soft sound of the pipes Pan plays. It's as if she is nine years old, alone in the forest, swaying and moving without fear or care. "What was in that wine?" she asks.

He chuckles and asks back, "What do you want to be in that wine?"

She pauses. "Answers — and nothing cryptic, please."

He scrutinizes her from head to toe and says, "The pond awaits you." Cindy undresses without hesitation and walks into the pond. Its water is dark, burnt-umber brown, and she can feel the mud squishing in between her toes. Cindy lets go and lies face down on the water in a dead woman's float. She drifts out to the center of the pond and feels a downward pull, like a rope is connected to her navel. As with suction, this rope pulls her down, down, down until she is one with the mud of the earth. Cindy lies in the mud and feels no need for air. She finds it incredibly relaxing not to worry about breathing. The earth is dark and womb-like. Cindy lies there quietly, enjoying the peace of this place and thinking that someday, this kind of peace would be with her above ground.

After a short eternity, Cindy swims up to the surface and takes a breath. She finds Pan ordering all sorts of creatures about to have the proper amount of abundance, especially grapes, for the bacchanalia. Cindy thinks presentation — no matter how muddy your life is — presentation is important. Unfortunately, her white Wranglers show it's been a while since they had been laundered, so she finds a field of Queen Anne's Lace and uses spiderwebs to adhere the flowers all over her white clothes. She wears white snowflakes of lace from head to toe. Cindy wraps her underwear in leaves as a party gift for Pan; her mother used to say, "Never show up empty-handed to a party."

As twilight passes and the cobalt blue of night disappears, it grows dark. Amidst this total blackness, fireflies appear by the thousands, everywhere. They are so dense, it was as if all the stars had come down to kiss the ground. With a wolflike howl, Pan lights the bonfire with a torch to begin the evening's festivities. Cindy is shy at parties, especially with so many foreign creatures around. Also, the fact that Pan's lovers have come to such unkindly ends makes her turn around and walk back to the highway.

There sits Karen, her reliable truck, waiting for Cindy to put it into gear. Cindy lifts her right hand up. Wind still from the south. She climbs in and finds champagne waiting for her on the passenger's side. The best kind of passenger, she thinks. CindySleigh puts her truck in first gear and peels out from the gravel, heading south on Route 611, feeling oddly like this is home.

Riding along, letting her trusty pickup steer their route, Cindy feels a restlessness coming upon her. Ah, my old friend, welcome. Show me the way. Cindy always needed to be in some sort of contact — to make things happen, though they never do. Karen locates a boxing gym and automatically pulls over. Cindy has heard of this place. As a chick, you can grease down, gear up, and get in the ring with a really big, well-built boxer. The rules are that he can move but not hit you. Cindy possesses more than an average girl's love of aggression. Sure, the rules are unfair, but what an opportunity for contact.

She goes in and is rubbed down with oil. She puts the bit in her mouth and the helmet on. White boxing gloves make it seem like they knew she was coming. All five foot nine inches, one hundred and thirty-five pounds of her enters through the ropes and into the ring. Sir would not approve. "I know I am not ready for this, but this place is here — not to mention a man — and I need to do this," she whispers to herself. To leverage her mind, she begins to breathe slowly. "Focus," Sir would say. Cindy has an odd habit of looking all over the room instead of at who she is talking to, always moving and not knowing what she is thinking most of the time. She is an invisible wave. When she was four, the kids would ask her, "Hey Cindy, whatcha doin'? Talkin' to the angels?"

Cindy knew that if a person looked into her eyes, they could see her thoughts and hear her heart. She learned early in life that love from humans can often be a very sharp, double-edged sword. All the years she studied with Sir, he was constantly on her to focus her mind, eyes, and ears. (Try it for an hour — it's really hard!) The man in the ring is beautiful, but all Cindy can see is injustice and humiliation, and all she feels is pure unadulterated anger. And it has to go somewhere.

This boxer's name is Jay. Normally, he feels kindly towards women, but he doesn't like this woman who looks more like an animal than a girl. Good thing she's a lightweight, too long and probably awkward to boot, he thinks as he sizes her up. Cindy recognizes this look of ennui that passes over Jay's eyes and immediately throws a powerful right jab. They have not yet started the round — clearly foul play. However, in Cindy's mind, it is one for all the people who have dismissed her in life.

The bell rings. They dance lightly on their feet, and Cindy, sometimes losing focus but never determination, throws the combinations Sir has taught her. Right, right-left, jab, hop step back, and jab again. She never hits Jay, not even once. He glides across the mat as though gravity has no effect on him whatsoever. He moves quickly but appears to be in slow motion, which infuriates Cindy. He plays with her like she is a puppy. Cindy decides to pull out all her feminine wiles, and in her usual awkwardness, she falls to the mat. He, forgetting everything, leans down to help her up; and she gives him an upper cut in the abs that he will never forget. Stunned, Jay takes her down with a cross to the jaw. Cindy feels the room swirling as she looks up at the ceiling from the mat. She's always liked that view. Ceilings are always so clean and empty. She tastes blood coming from her lip and smiles broadly. Jay smiles, too. He does not, however, reach down to help her up from the mat. Cindy rolls over and does ten push-ups to clear her head. Then she stands up, laughing out loud. "Thanks, Jay, that was swell." Jay leans forward and cautiously kisses her white boxing gloves.

Cindy walks away and heads for the showers. It has been a while, so she spends a good hour under the steaming hot water, scrubbing herself down like she is scouring a floor. She makes sure she still has skin wrapped around her when she is done. The intensity of the fight reminds her of what *alive*, really alive, can be. Where each moment is like an hour and each movement means something. Really hot water is truly a gift, she thinks as she drinks some down and spits some out mixed with blood onto the tiles.

As she leaves the gym, Cindy feels ready for more. More of what, she's not sure. Trusty Karen flashes her lights so

Cindy can find the black Chevy pickup truck in the parking lot. Cindy climbs in, checks out her fat lip in the rear view mirror, smiles at herself, and heads south.

The many hours of the night speed by as CindySleigh drives south, but she is not present. In her mind, she creates a drawing, a self-portrait, graphite on paper: in a frontal stance, perfectly calm and normal, although her chest is open to expose her heart. No bone, muscle, or skin protect it from all of the feelings and emotions that spin around her like a whirlwind. This self-image makes sense. In it, as throughout her entire life, her eyes are askew.

In her art studio, she could express all her feelings without exposing herself to the world. People were always too confusing and often mean. It was much safer in the studio. Here the world belonged to Cindy, and she could create whatever she wanted her world to be. When Cindy was lost in desire and adopted the abused D.C., it never occurred to her that her love would not only be rejected but that D.C. would see her open heart, zero in on it, and using jabs, left hooks, upper cuts — every punch he could muster — hit her, strike her with his words, extracting pain every day and night.

Despite litany, repeated catechism, Father Michael could not protect Cindy from D.C. She began to remove herself from Father Michael, too, because he proved a new source of pain. She felt alone. For seven years until the day she left, July 17th, 2007, Cindy had endured all she could.

Was her heart salvageable from all of these beatings? Without a heart, there is no life; without pain, there is no life.

The sun peeks out as if frightened of the day, and Cindy suddenly lurches back into the present. She is driving Karen, heading soth. She looks up and sees a sign welcoming her to New Hope. She remembers the town from her teenage years, listening to Jeff Claflin play in a piano bar, acting older than her years. Cindy wonders what remains in the New Hope of today.

First things first, she parks Karen. Next, presentation. Cindy finds her way easily around New Hope, stopping by a shop and buying a two-layer cotton-gauze sleeveless dress, nude in color, cut to the waist in the front. She buys flesh-colored ballet slippers to match. Then, around the corner, she floats into the local spa and intensely focuses during an hour-long hot oil massage. The message keeps her mind from drifting. "And I thought massages were supposed to do the opposite," she thinks. The hot eucalyptus steam bath makes her sweat, as though every river she has crossed on her journey runs down her body. Afterwards, a woman scrubs her down with a rough loofah, using a mixture that smells like a combination of wood and maple syrup. Feeling only this side of being completely transparent, Cindy glides into the hair salon and has her crew cut turned into a nude color to match her skin and her dress. Underwear is no longer necessary, as she is nakedly clothed. Cindy feels color and vibrancy all around her as she walks down the streets of New Hope, only half visible. She spots Manon, a *Provençal* French restaurant with Crayola crayon colors on its exterior walls. "Perfect, I can totally disappear in there," she tells herself. She waltzes in, literally, sits at the bar and orders champagne: Veuve Cliquot, in honor of the widow Cliquot who survived by creating a great champagne. The color of the champagne matches her skin, her dress, her hair, and her shoes. CindySleigh feels so transparent, she is sure the bartender can see the bubbles traveling down her throat, dispersing through her bloodstream, and changing even the color of her blood. "I almost do not exist," she muses. Her pain momentarily subsides as she swallows yet again.

Cindy scans the room. Details of Van Gogh paintings have been recreated on each wall; *Starry Night* swirls across the ceiling. The colors pulsate. She can feel someone behind her. Marc enters the room. He is the muse sent by the gods to emanate goodness so we somehow can continue. He looks at no one as he intently prepares to play his music. The piano resounds as emotion fills the room with the love with which he plays. As if in a trance, he begins to sing of SUVs, of people loving, living, and dying, all while dancing. Somehow, the entire great wheel of life is presented, not as serious, but rather as a carefree wheel, the Ferris wheel, as a pureness comes through his voice. He is dressed to please himself, which makes Cindy smile. When he sings of talking all night and everything still being the same in the morning, she feels the truth of it.

He does not see Cindy sitting at the bar, as he is captured in his moment, aside from the fact that she is only half there, being transparent. The crowd applauds. His songs touch them, and they feel, for a slice of an hour, awake. He looks up, and Cindy acknowledges the odd directness of his green eyes upon her. She smiles, not knowing if she is visible at this point. With his taller-bigger-from-who-I-am-inside appearance, he strides towards her. She cannot help but admire his striking beauty, his lovely curls, and his Converse sneakers.

"Hi, Cindy. Hold my hand. Come back to solid so we can chat." She does as she is told. She holds his hand and her veins start pumping, her hand becoming visible. "Hand the bartender a credit card, wouldya? I'm not sure he knows I am here," Cindy whispers.

"Sure," he replies, ordering a Shirley Temple for himself. Cindy decides to be casual. She can never tell what Marc's been thinking, as his eyes only reflect; he is an observer par excellence.

"I was wondering if you would take a look at my cards," she asks. "They have taken an odd turn." Marc is a master reader of the Tarot cards. He is an expert at seeing the unforeseen. Cindy herself avoids the future at all costs, as every step in that direction feels like falling off a steep cliff.

"Sure, Cindy. Let's take a look," Marc responds. She unwraps her cards. She slowly shuffles through them. Yep, still all the Two of Swords, but now, the woman does not even possess the swords anymore. Only empty hands, card after card. She hands the deck to Marc, inaction culminating to this point in time. He sips his Shirley Temple without even looking at the cards, then smiles at her, and holds her hand for a few minutes, aware she is disappearing on him again.

He pulls her significator card which proves to be incredibly significant: the Two of Swords. There she is, blindfolded, but at least her swords are back. "Damn, I bet the rest of the reading will be the same," Cindy says with doubt. As Marc turns over the four cards of the Celtic cross, the cards transform themselves: the Ten of Pentacles, the Page of Swords, the Star, and the Wheel of Fortune. Cindy's head is caught in the wheel, as it has been for the last seven years. It has been a long time since her deck was as it should be. It almost does not matter what the cards mean; the fact that other aspects exist makes her glow. Maybe hope isn't just something Hallmark marketed like Soma to the masses. The wheel is turning quickly in her head.

Marc, on the other hand, cries out when he pulls the Two of Swords for Cindy. It was as if this card were something brand new.

Cindy seems to be gathering more solidity, though she is not really thinking about it. Her mind races: "Oh my God, I have more than one card, more than one fate. Perhaps the future does exist." Then she falters, fading quickly. "How could it be so? I know we are who we are, this is not a choice."

Marc grabs her hand to keep her in this world and asserts, "You are the wheel of fortune. It is out there. A steering wheel in a black Chevy pickup named Karen." Having to steer her own future becomes evident to Cindy. Marc speaks of a great sense of bounty in her past, clear in the Ten of Pentacles card. Marc keeps talking to retain Cindy in the world of possibility, reminding her that people who love you are always with you, even when they are absent. She finds it hard to incorporate absent love, but she'll give it a shot.

Cindy concentrates on breathing. Breathing is a conscious effort for her. Eventually, her fate solidifies, and CindySleigh knows where she has to go: 2957 Old Welsh Road. To the house her dad built, where magic appeared every day without any effort whatsoever.

Cindy and Marc stand up together and hug the open hug of love. Hugging Marc is special, as Cindy rests her chin on his left shoulder, hanging out there, taking all that good in. "You are the star that leads me," she whispers as she quickly kisses him on the cheek and runs out the door.

Marc quietly smiles and finishes his Shirley Temple.

The pickup moves at a clip like a horse that knows the way home. Cindy looks out the window, observing Pennsylvania. Unlike the flat desert beach and marshland of New Jersey, Pennsylvania has a pastoral quality of timelessness: open spaces under the trees, rounded boulders appearing out of the ground, and hills that hold you where they touch and meet each other.

The truck stops. CindySleigh glances up. "How did we get on Route 309?" she wonders. There she is, in front of Plymouth-Whitemarsh Cemetery. Cindy puts the pickup in first gear. The cemetery gates open, and she coasts in and parks in guest parking. Feeling only half like a guest, she proceeds across the grass. There are no headstones here, only beautifully, perfectly mowed lime-green lawns with rectangular plaques geometrically placed along the ground. Cindy peers down; Frank and Ella, her parents, together underground. It has been almost twenty years since Cindy was here. She had stopped by once before to make sure the copper plate trimmed with oak leaves for her parents had actually been delivered. Sitting cross-legged on the ground, she thinks, perhaps in the spirit of the Mexican Day of the Dead, that she should update — no, just talk to — her ancestors who died so young and lived so earnestly.

"Hi," she utters shyly. "I am still up here. I thought

about taking up your offer of the empty plot next to you, but I decided to pass for now. I must learn to be more patient. Death comes to everyone. No need to hurry it along. I hope you are holding hands down there. I miss you very much. Why haven't you helped me with D.C.? You were always just so big and all. You were always so big, so vibrant and young. You did not live long enough to become frail. Death stole you from me too soon. I am so stuck." Then she heard her dad's laugh. That big booming laugh that always made all of Cindy's anxieties disappear. Cindy laughs, too. Nothing ever really does change, even though it seems to. Every day is the same day. She abruptly stands. It was odd to hear a laugh from the dead. Cindy, about to run back to the truck, instead takes a minute to think. Then she lies down next to her parents on the ground, yearning to feel the peace she imagines death would be. The sky is perfectly clear, and she lets its pure blue saturate her eyes as she remains still. Suddenly, with her peripheral vision, she sees a table and chair. Cindy immediately thinks of Thornton Wilder's play *Our Town*, and sits up, ready for anything. If the dead can laugh, who knows what else can happen.

Cindy's mother is sitting at the table playing solitaire. Cindy sits across from her and watches. (Watching her play solitaire was a regular pastime for CindySleigh. Cindy has inherited many of her mother's secretive ways.) Cindy cannot tell what her mom is thinking about while she methodically places one card over another. Silence holds the Queen of Hearts in place as Cindy watches in awe. Then Ella, in her typical fashion, leans over, reaches down to the ground, and picks a four-leafed clover. She sits up, looks at Cindy with a slight smile, and hands it to her. Cindy just gazes at it in her hand. When she looks up, her mother is no longer there. The vacuum of death is repeated.

Cindy hears people and notices another table under a tree. She gets up and walks over, finding her father, Uncle Fred, Uncle Maurice, Uncle George, and of course Aunt Marie, who would never sit with the women when there was pinochle to be played. Uncle George deals out the cards, and each of them has a beer by their side. Uncle Fred begins humming and soon they are all singing as they rearrange their hands to begin a round. Cindy experiences a new vision of the afterlife. Unlike Thornton Wilder's self-righteous dead who sit so still, so above the living, Cindy is seeing life in death. Perhaps death is continuous moments of one's life at its best, shining in the light of day. Maybe the afterlife is a picnic on a Sunday. Aunt Marie slams down a card and wins the round. The men complain. Aunt Marie laughs and downs her beer. Cindy hears the screech of Karen's horn and turns around; when she looks back at her parent's plot only the tree and grass remain.

Cindy scans the horizon, but there are no other people, no further visions in sight. She is alone in the landscape of the dead. Cindy quietly walks to her truck and climbs in. She notices her left hand is clenched. Opening it, she discovers a four-leaf clover. Time is relative, she decides, and relatives are with me in time. It was comforting to see them again. CindySleigh feels grateful. These people gave her laughter, singing, and many small but meaningful moments of joy. Now it was time to head home.

Route 611, Limekiln Pike, Easton Road. As the Romans said, all roads lead to Rome. In Cindy's life, all roads seem to lead home. The house Cindy grew up in is where the black truck heads next. 2957 Old Welsh Road, just off Route 611. Cindy parks out front and waits. Her ever-ready bottle of champagne appears, and she sits very still, sipping the elixir of nightmares and dreams. Frank and Ella, with all of their brothers and sisters, and Grandma and Grandpop camped out each weekend while building this house. Cindy's dad was a big man, six feet three inches tall, size thirteen triple-E shoes. His pinkie ring was way too big for Cindy's thumb. His hands and voice were huge and so were his anger and his laughter. He was always bigger than a mere human could be. Frank would tell Cindy stories about building the house: they felled forty trees and one of them fell on her cousin, but his legs were fine because it had rained so much he just sank into the mud (big loud laugh).

There was one story she loved the most, the one that made her an artist. Dad told her that when digging the foundation of the house, they unearthed two huge boulders and did not know what to do with them. Then he realized the back porch was raised up, soon to be enclosed. All of the men pushed the boulders under the back porch and sealed them in with concrete blocks. There they remain, under the porch, never to see the light of day, behind the white stucco surface. Cindy wonders about the real that is not seen but that you know is there. Or is it? Of all the things she would do this day, she is surely going to sledgehammer the side of the porch and see if it's true, to see if the hidden can see the light of day. Or, is it only magic if it stays hidden? "I will wipe out this conundrum with many blows," she affirms to herself out loud.

The house, a white stucco, two-story home (one story never finished), displays an immense gothic "S" on the fireplace chimney, a small, fake wishing well on the front lawn, and a curving, many-colored slate walk leading to the front door. This place held the core of Cindy's heart; she's not sure she ever really left. The oak tree in the front is now twice the size of the house. Father Michael helped her dad plant it as a sapling, when the priest was still a young man. You can count on nature to continue to grow and thrive in its seemingly random abandon of constant proliferation of whatever works now. Can't we be more that way? The house stands empty and abandoned. Cindy walks up the sandy driveway, picking up pieces of rose quartz and mica on her way to the back door, which opens easily. This did not surprise her as the door was always left unlocked.

First things first. Cindy heads down to the basement. As she steps down each stair, the wet smell of dirt and the coolness of underground, all that makes basements scary but enticing places, comes upon her. Cindy scans the space, searching for something — she does not know what. She grabs one of the cold cement posts they used to swing around while roller skating there. She views the area her brother used to paint in, the remains of the paintings on the floor. She smiles at the pinball machine they had totally dismantled when she was young; the guts proved so much more interesting than the game. Next, she eyes the big red boiler. She opens the small square where the ashes would wind up from the fireplace upstairs. Ashes remained there. Frank's tools lay everywhere, spread out in chaos about the empty spot where he had died on the cement floor. She scans the tools and finds his sledgehammer. She picks it up.

Cindy turns her back and climbs the stairs. She feels as if she is coming up out of the ground. She opens the back door and throws the sledge hammer onto the driveway. Cindy returns for her journey into the main floor of the house. Not a long journey, as all childhood houses shrink as we grow up. She finds herself heading for the bedrooms, the places where dreams actually occur. Her brother's room is still a conflation of boats and planes on the wallpaper, with counterfeit diamonds casually tossed upon the bed. Ceramic mallard ducks continue to fly across the wall. All is in exactly same spot as then. Just like

CindySleigh.

Cindy closes the door and walks into the bedroom she shared with her sister, Nanny. She sees the familiar wallpaper of delicate pink-and-white dogwood on a light-turquoise field. The gray-painted bureaus are still covered with butterfly decals. Two double windows look out onto the front yard. The mimosa tree is in full bloom, its flowers like peach-decorated wishes. Through a rear window, she sees the backyard, with its massive borders of peonies — fuchsia, pink and white — falling over with heavy, hearty blooms. There they remain poised before the mighty maple and beech trees that fill the rest of the window view with vibrant, lush green. To this day, the importance of a room often stems from what Cindy can see out its window to the world.

Cindy turns away and walks into the bathroom, white and aqua blue. Cindy cannot take her eyes off the six-foot white bathtub. It was so big that, as a child, she could levitate on the water without touching any solid surface, floating freely as if on the sea. Entering the hallway, she looks to her left to peek into her parent's bedroom. Cindy was not allowed in there. Her iPod sings, "Don't know where I'm goin', don't know where I've been."

Cindy decides to go into the sacred bedroom of her parents with its heavy mahogany furniture. She eyes her mother's vanity lamps: white porcelain figurines, detailed in silver, of a man and a woman in 19th-century garb. White lampshades hover over the pair like fancy hats. Wherever Cindy was, if she saw lights remotely similar, she would feel the tug of home. Things are so powerful in this way, so sturdy in the air and in our minds.

Cindy opens the top drawer of her mother's bureau, revealing a mixture of old nylons, iridescent baubles, ivory gloves, and fake jewels. She leans down and inhales her mother's face powder. Cindy cries. Pulling herself away, she opens her dad's nightstand and finds over 500 golf pencils amidst random socks. He never threw anything away. Instead, he would bring the discards of other people's lives home, thinking it would fill his own.

Cindy did not have trouble throwing things away but could not rid herself of the lifelong burden of feelings that were killing her from the inside out. Her feelings were as solid and heavy as the boulders hidden under the back porch.

As she wanders into the living room, Cindy smells smoke. Her footprints, as she looks back, smolder and ignite into fire. While memory burns into your brain and heart, trapped in the moment, its trace does not yet exist. At this second, she begins to feel the actual sequence of time. She longs for the concrete feeling of eventuality to become her reality. She is in the present; the reality of this thought is *fire* to Cindy. Fire cleanses the way. The house is burning! She must get out.

Cindy quietly walks out the back door and down the stairs. She focuses herself, grabs the sledgehammer, and carefully aims at the side of the back porch.

What she left me Nadel

THE SINKING
SHIP

CHAPTER ONE

Buying & Selling

Cindy walked across an imaginary line and entered Mexico, a step that led her into the usual cacophony of a border town. Quickly, she found herself surrounded by countless five-year-old beggars. Poor, undernourished children set out in droves to sell their caramel candy. Immersed in poverty, the men in the stalls called out to Cindy, "If we do not have what you want we will steal it for you." Believing the worst of themselves, they did the ugliness that others projected. *No gracias, no gracias, no gracias* became her mantra for the day as she scanned back and forth to absorb her surroundings. Cindy looked for objects to bring home, but buying and selling were not just material ends for her. The interchange seemed full of portent, and there was always the potential for human contact. As she wandered about following her radar, the men kept haranguing her. Cindy did not mind, understanding the meager circumstances that put them in this space and time.

Out of her left eye she saw a silent stall, where she glanced upon painted metal — textured, primitively cut, rubbed with blue paint. A fish leapt up to her from the wall from which it hung. She stopped and met a silver-haired gentleman with round, black wire-rimmed glasses. "¿Me llamo Faustino, y usted?"

"Me llamo Cindy." Faustino and Cindy nodded to each other and proceeded to speak in a mix of broken English and Spanish. Fluidly, they moved with ease past each other, speaking and touching each magical creation he had made, to find just the right six pieces for her friends. Cindy began with the fish, then added a moon, a rose, and a butterfly or *mariposa* as he called it. Cindy laughed with delight to learn the meaning of her friend Sybil's last name.

"Animales," Faustino repeated over and over throughout his small booth, searching for exactly the right pieces. Discovering they shared the love of making things, he showed her his metals, his pattern-making tools, and his paint. "Happiness, sadness, they are like the weather. They come and they go. However, do beware of what you ask for, señora. When you seek, spirits see you and things happen. Things you do not expect and can no longer control," Faustino warned. Then, as quickly as a dark cloud passes by, his face changed. "I know what you are; you are a teacher," he said. CindySleigh smiled at the compliment but shook her head no. She asked Faustino for *milagros* of sacred hearts for her sacred friends, and he left her briefly, climbing into a trailer nearby. He returned to tell Cindy, "They are away, traveling. We must only have our own hearts to count on today."

THEY DID NOT notice the sun moving behind the clouds, and, suddenly, all of the long shadows of day's end surrounded them. As Faustino carefully wrapped Cindy's fantasy world in newspaper, a deeper shadow passed over his face. "Mi amigo, what is it?" Cindy inquired.

"Darkness comes in many forms. It is my duty to ask you about it," Faustino haltingly said. Cindy looked all around, thinking about messengers sent from the spirits. "This seems like the kind of place I would hide out in if I were a spirit," Cindy mused. Lost in the familiar exchange of buying and selling, she wondered about Faust and his barter with the devil. Faustino's name was a bit unnerving, as she knew well the plight of Faust. Just reading the poem could put you in a tailspin. On the other hand, she had already experienced life's eternity and damnation, so Cindy decided to walk forward, to see what would happen.

Cindy turned and looked Faustino in the eyes. His face became very serious as he said, "Un momento, señora." He turned around and looked at the faded cloth hanging behind his wares at the back of the booth. Cindy felt the temperature drop and shivered. From behind the curtain came a beautiful man, dressed entirely in black leather. "An advertisement for my trade," he explained as Cindy openly scanned him from head to toe. It was all about black. He would do well in Manhattan, with men and women, Cindy thought. He wore a black leather cowboy hat with a slight indigo tinge, perfectly matching his eyes, where the retina melted into the iris to make dark pools the color of the night sky. Cindy did not dare look away. The air was a circus act, flipping and turning. Danger! Sexy, earthy, scary, fun? She was not sure. He wore black leather chaps over his leather pants. His boots seemed oddly small for his size, shining as if made of dark glass. Beautiful flames of fire — red, orange, and gold circled around them. Faustino, looking a little pale, said nothing. Cindy extended her hand: "I am CindySleigh."

"I know," he said. As they grasped hands, a psychic tug of war began. Looking at each other's eyes, neither one of them would let go. It was as though rivers of information were being passed through their palms. "I was wondering if I could shine your boots," he asked. She could not believe this came out of his mouth. She should have remembered: to serve is to lead, but she did not. The leather chaps overwhelmed her senses.

Cindy responded, "How much?" as she regained some sense of clarity.

"Well that depends," he replied.

"Okay," she managed to whisper, thinking stupid, stupid, stupid.

Faustino cleared his throat and lifted the tattered curtain that led to the back. Cindy found herself in an empty room, dirt for a floor, a small straight-back chair, and a wooden crate with a bare light bulb hanging over it. Remembering what her teacher had taught her, she never turned her back to the man in black. This took some negotiating, even in an empty room, and she found herself breathing deeply from her belly. "I did not catch your name," Cindy said.

"When you shine shoes, what does a name matter? Call me what you will, señora," the man in black answered. "In fact, besides shining your white leather boots, your will is something we could perhaps discuss." A Tarot card flashed a message behind her eyes: El Diablo. He nodded in recognition as though he could read her mind, very unsettling for CindySleigh. She did not like how transparent she appeared to him. Closing her feelings and ideas off to outsiders was something Cindy had been working very hard to perfect in the last six months, and evidently she had not been too successful. The devil did not frighten her, as each side in life, she knew, must have an opposite side: ideas, nature, people, animals, coins. It was the fact that he could see into her that frightened her.

Cindy sat down, put her left leg up on the wooden crate in front of her, rolled her pant leg up to her knee and said nothing. She watched him lay out his tools on the left side of the crate: oils, brushes, soft cloths. When he opened the polish, she sensed the smell of animals permeate the room. Then he sat down. All this time, Cindy was focused, prepared, excited, and frightened. Who would think that one could feel all that while having boots shined? As she stared, Cindy became absolutely convinced that this was Mephistopheles. He had all the time of time and moved with the grace you learn living in eternity. Temptation, quite an art form, was something he had obviously practiced. Distance was what Cindy should have been cultivating at this point, but instead, she just watched him shine her boots with loving concentration. "You provide quite a service, señor," she commented.

"Ah, my lovely lady, there is nothing short of the world I would not do for you," and he smiled a broad smile. His teeth were glistening. Buffing her boot just below her knee, he leaned within four inches of her face and whispered, "What do you want?" Their eyes were connected with imaginary tunnels; she did not reply.

He leaned back and sighed while slowly gathering up all his tools and putting them away. Cindy rolled down her jeans, leaned toward Mephistopheles, and said, "What can you offer me?" He stared straight at Cindy, not answering her with words.

As if speaking to him out loud, she silently mused: "Since you see behind my eyes, señor, you already know desire will not incite me to sell my soul. I have found and lost it many times already. I have experienced enough in this one lifetime to know better than to wish and dream.

Dreams always have an underbelly, not always spoken of, but often a source of regret. I know that each human embodies many souls. Selling you one is perhaps not so important. Your terms must be much more tempting than they were for Faust. I am not asking for guidance. I like to work on my journey. I do not like help. I like to discover in my own way, though I do find you intriguing. The animal in me is very wary. Still, the human in me is curious as to what you might say, ask, or do."

The two of them parted ways, with Cindy carefully backing out of the room and away from the man in black. She pushed aside the worn cloth, only to be bathed in the light of a full moon. Faustino's booth was nowhere to be seen. When she looked at the ground, there lay her six animals, carefully folded in newspaper. She picked the parcel up and walked away. Cindy knew that this had been her first but would not be the last encounter with he whose true name we dare not speak, as it reminds us too much of the darkest part of ourselves.

CHAPTER TWO

The Author Meets Him

Mephistopheles walked away from town into the foothills surrounding Nogales. He took a step back as the Author appeared in front of him. "Well, hello, señora, I was not expecting you. What a treat! One is not often surprised in eternity," he said.

"I saw you talking to CindySleigh, you snake. She does not always share with me, so I thought it best to go right to the source that is surely going to cause her pain." The Author mimicked Cindy's penchant for low eye contact. She needed to protect Cindy. The Author was behaving more bravely than she felt.

"Now, just hold on a minute here, I was just shining her boots," he said with one of his more charming smiles.

"Stop that. I hate charm. It never involves the whole truth. It is much more like half a truth with a bit of seduction thrown in. *Yuck*." The Author immediately regretted her honest knee-jerk reaction. Mephistopheles is Mephistopheles. This was not the time to overreact; it was the time to use tact. He could extinguish life with the snap of his fingertips.

El Diablo checked himself out in a mirror that suddenly appeared in his hand, as if he did not hear a word the

Author had said. Even though he admired himself fully, there was no image reflected. The Author realized she was involved in a game where magic was sleight of hand, but the sleight of hand did not explain the magic.

"Look, I have been watching Cin, as I like to refer to her, for quite a while now. Face it," he said, as he turned the hand mirror to the Author's face. "She is bored as hell," he continued, laughing at his own joke.

Wordless, the Author pushed the mirror away.

He continued, "Maybe hell would be a step up from the arid desert I see inside of her. We both know CindySleigh is in need of a challenge. She is restless as ... well, you know what I mean." Mephistopheles looked at the Author until she returned his gaze. She was not so unlike CindySleigh. Without blinking, he scanned her with those two navy-black eyes that see behind what you decide to show.

The Author could not immediately think of what to say. She wanted to protect Cindy yet knew that what he had said about Cindy was true. The Author took a step back, as all authors must, and asked, "What is it that you propose, sir?"

As the Author retreated from Mephistopheles' stare, an entire picnic spread out before them. All the food came from various forms of apple. Out of her peripheral vision, she saw the fast-moving small gray snakes that had prepared this feast, quickly slithering away.

"How should I refer to you, señora?" El Diablo asked as they sat on the soft red-and-white checkered cloth.

"I, like you, sir, have no actual spoken name. I am referred to as the Author."

"Have a nice glass of apple wine, dear author," the dark spirit suggested, although it sounded more like a very softly spoken command.

The Author held up the glass, drinking without memory of having ever picked it up. She was clearly out of her league here. She got her bearings — ground, sky, left hand holding glass, as though reciting the actuality of concrete objects would save her from the inevitable: whatever he could conjure with the dip of his eyelashes.

"You will see in your dreams, dear author, that since you have already seen the truth with me, I need not confer with you as to my plans." Those were the last words the Author heard as she fell into a slumber so deep and calm, it was as if she were surrounded, underneath and on all sides, by the feathers of birds.

* * *

THE AUTHOR STOOD on the sand by the ocean. She heard a voice say, *"Boca de cielo,"* the mouth of heaven. As white as the sand was, it made her eyes tear, and she had to keep covering them with her hands. She turned to look out at the sea, acid green, black, tumultuous, and threatening. Confused, the Author looked back and forth. Nothing here seemed heavenlike.

Mephistopheles was standing under a rectangular gazebo. The Author ran to him to escape the intensity of the place.

"How could the mouth of heaven be this?" she asked.

El Diablo scanned the horizon with ease. "It does not look the same to each person. I see what you see: heaven, hell, life. Too intense for you, is it?"

"But I want it all," the Author pleaded. Afraid the spirit did not understand, she repeated as she covered her eyes, "¡Quiero todo el Mundo!"

"That is not what you are showing me in your dream. The sea of emotion is far from calm, and the goodness around you is blinding. There is so much, it literally blinds you, and you cannot see it or really take it in. You are a blind author full of regret. Let CindySleigh go. The journey is hers and hers alone."

* * *

THE AUTHOR WOKE up with a start, jumped up, and stood in a fighting stance. She found herself alone in an apple orchard. She relaxed and looked around. She remembered being worried about something or someone. The Author picked an apple off of the tree and bit into it. It was bittersweet.

CHAPTER THREE

Black

Walking away in the cool of the night, parcel in hand, Cindy was a blank slate inside and out. She was becoming the shadow the moonlight cast of her once solid self, and soon the magical animals would slip from her hands. Shadows cannot hold on to anything; they just move and mimic life. Being a shadow did not seem to bother CindySleigh as she wandered out into a landscape that became more and more barren. The empty space with a moving shadow, so much like a moving painting. Sand made a great negative space for the shape and figure of Cindy's shadow as she danced in the desert. Soon, sleep sought her out. She lay down, in line with the shadow of an evergreen tree, so if somebody or some nonbody were walking about, they would be less apt to step on her. Instead of quiet sleep, dreams fell down on top of her.

* * *

A WOMAN LITERALLY fell on top of Cindy, complaining about the sea being chartreuse and black, saying something about the stark white, bleached brightness of life. She covered her eyes and shook all over. Cindy's shadow wrapped itself around the solid woman to soften the bright light and calm her seas. They slowly settled in and slept together like spoons, with the shadow of the evergreen tree protecting them from the "other than."

THE "OTHER THAN" was there, watching, waiting; Mephistopheles never sleeps. It is a habit he gave up many eons ago, as he could nightmare while awake, making sleep an afterthought. He sat nearby, wondering how the Author had made it back to Cindy. The Author was a determined sort, and they did look sort of cute, lying there together: one solid and pragmatic but so lost in her concreteness; the other full of unexpected thoughts, accepting all change and constantly morphing, not knowing one moment from the next. As he was sitting full of thought, the early glow of the next day settled in, and he saw the spirit of the Author begin to separate from the shadow of CindySleigh. The Author could not hold onto shadow. She floated up into the air. Her body dividing into pieces of jigsaw puzzle. He saw her try to will her pieces together, but the Author was unprepared for this place of dreams. Her will was not strong enough to keep herself together — or with Cindy. The pieces of the Author scattered and disappeared. All this while CindySleigh continued to hug her shadow-self, fast asleep.

Mephistopheles reached into Cindy's subconscious while she slept. "There must be something in there I can use to begin to tie her to me," he thought. While rumbling around in Cindy's mind, he came upon a very happy greyhound that immediately began barking, trying to wake her up. This devil really did have a smile, taking true joy in his more than mischievous makings.

He stood back and put two fingers in his mouth, using the silent whistle, meant for Black. Even Mephistopheles had a need for comfort. The silent whistle brought his familiar. A jumping, barking black dog appeared by his side. Black was a mid-size Australian wild dog with one problem: his tail would not stay attached. It kept flying about near him but hardly ever on him. Black did not see this as a problem because trying to catch it with his teeth gave him endless sport. His canine teeth glistened like his master's.

The greyhound in Cindy's mind just had to come out and play. From shadow to greyhound was not really that big a transformation, at least not in Cindy's world. Both Cindy, as a greyhound, and Black, the wild dog, looked at each other with surprise. They expressed their joy, which involved much jumping about and running in circles. Then CindySleigh noticed Black's tail flying about and quickly but gently jumped. She lifted all four legs, caught it with grace, and nuzzled it back in place. They circled and sniffed each other as dogs do, then they spotted a rabbit and took off.

As you already know, Cindy loves to run. She bounded forward and leaned into the wind, filled with rapture that had nothing to do with the rabbit. She actually passed the rabbit and just kept going, but then she noticed her new companion was no longer with her. CindySleigh turned around to find Black tearing apart the rabbit. Blood was everywhere. Soon, blood was all that was left. Black wagged his newly attached tail at Cindy, but the greyhound did not move. Her instincts were watching. She was not sure of her new friend.

Of course, Mephistopheles, lying in the desert grass, was also watching, always looking for that second, that miniscule lapse, to capture some leak, some part of you hidden from yourself. He saw his initial doorway beginning to close when Cindy surprised him by coming forward to Black. She began cleaning all of the blood off of him with her tongue. With each lick, she tried to clean the darkness from El Diablo's dog. Black could not really think, but he knew this felt good. He did not pull away, and Cindy cleaned him head to tail. By now the sun was high, so they wandered over to the shadow of a big rock and circled around several times, as dogs do, before they settled in next to each other for a nap.

CHAPTER FOUR

White

CindySleigh stretched her arms out as far as she could, returning from the land of dreams. Her eyes were still closed when she felt something hairy under her right arm. "Oh God, what did I get myself into now," she thought, assuming it was a very hairy man. Cindy was surprised when she finally opened her eyes to find a beautiful black dog under her right arm. His hair was so shiny, so black it shined blue. She began to stroke him softly, and he rolled over so his belly was up and his pink tongue hung out to the side. Compliant, Cindy rubbed his belly, and Black relished her attention.

El Diablo sat, lurking silently near, taking in all the playfulness of the two without interfering. True life entertainment was in short supply this century. By deploying electronic toys, he had blocked seventy-five percent of all genuine contact between humans. This made his work easier; however, it made observing humans much less fun. Animals could not fall into the virtual world. Black he kept, enjoying any sign of life, and here it appeared as budding friendship between his dog and Cindy. He wondered if he shouldn't just let her be. She was mostly spirit, so he would only be getting a small portion of a regular human soul. Mephistopheles cast these foreign thoughts away. The devil's work had to be done. He observed the fabric of CindySleigh. It had holes that had been resewn and repaired; the fabric was whole, but as in all lives, scars remain.

Cindy looked up from the ground to see Mephistopheles smiling at her. "I see you like my dog," he laughed heartily. Cindy stood up, brushed the dust off of her white Wranglers, and looked up at him with a scowl.

"Cin, you should smile more, it becomes you, and who knows what you would become if you did," he said through his own laughter. Black sat up and leaned against Cindy's leg as she petted him behind the ear.

Cindy ignored Mephistopheles' comment. "Only you could misshape the heart of an innocent animal. From now on, he stays with me so I can lessen his darkness," Cindy asserted.

Mephistopheles thought how easy this would be. He took one step forward. "What is this about, all these white clothes? Are you some kind of virgin or something?" he taunted.

Cindy took a step back. "I am a virgin of sorts, for no matter how many lovely, sordid sexual things I have done in this lifetime, I could never create a child. Forbidden fruits, I have no problem eating, chewing, and swallowing. Vases are beautiful in and of themselves, but there is something so much better when they are filled with flowers; even one flower would make all the difference. I wear my insides on my outside as I have nothing to hide. This keeps me from harm's way, usually. In your case, I am not so sure," Cindy said. She shifted from leg to leg as she realized she had revealed a longing. This was very dangerous territory.

Mephistopheles displayed no reaction. He was a good listener and knew that every human heart that lives longs. His magic was already in process: as the color of Black's fur began to lighten, CindySleigh's clothes grayed until the two matched completely. "It would be child's play to allow this to come to you," he plainly said.

Cindy immediately went into a fighting stance, loosening up with a few jabs before replying, "Don't bring any of that *Rosemary's Baby* nonsense to me. You, just keep your distance and stay exactly, and I mean *exactly*, where you are."

"What makes you so sure Black is a dog, anyway? You, of all people, Cindy, should recognize the ease of shape-shifting." All the while, the internal mutterings of ancient alchemies and the secret realignments of DNAs were in progress.

THEY STARED AT each other, Cindy with her fists up and Mephistopheleles softly rubbing his hands together as if they were slightly cold. His lips moved only as much as a tremble. By now, night was fully upon them, and when El Diablo stood still, his white teeth shining, Cindy knew immediately something was very wrong-right-confusing. She noticed Black's hand on her calf, but dogs do not have hands.

Cindy looked down to see a six-year-old boy clinging to her leg. He was still the wild animal that was there a moment ago. He leaned on her with all his weight and looked up to her with large burnt-umber eyes. It was a color that looked like he had been through a fire and survived. His head was a tumble of beautiful curls falling all about. The boy reminded her of the *putti* in Renaissance paintings, their short wings flying about. He looked at her steadily. His body was a bit thin for a cherub and full of too much life for his age.

It was too late for Cindy to choose; this boy was hers and hers alone from that time on. She looked up at Mephistopheles. Cindy knew in her mind that nothing could go well when devised by this spirit, the tails side of a copper penny incarnate. But CindySleigh also had a heart, and she figured it would carry her through the loss of her soul, enabling her to help this small boy.

The wind began to howl. It created small tornadoes around Cindy, and the sand spun around her and the small child. She took off her now-gray jacket to shield his nakedness from the stinging sand. Whether Mephistopheles was there, Cindy could not tell. She could not see more than one foot ahead of her. She picked the small boy up and began to walk; their direction was directionless, as there was no way she could see where they were headed, let alone what would happen next. Cindy knew only the weight of this small boy against her body, as he literally clung to her for life. Cindy had no gauge of time, but in time, the world became quieter.

Together, they gathered dried wood and built a fire. Having no matches, they hugged until a spark appeared flying to ignite the dried wood. Cindy and the wild one sat across from each other, sometimes staring into the flames, quietly noting this momentous change in their lives.

"I don't think Black will work out well in town," Cindy said. "I shall have to think. You need a new name. A demon brought you to me, and now you are the child I am going to take care of. How about D.C.?"

The small child observed her from across the flames. He simply replied, "Good." D.C. said good to everything, for up to this point in his life, nothing was good. From then on, even if things were bad, they were good. That is how bad bad can be.

Cindy watched him chew on his nails. She watched him pee and defecate without care, as if he enjoyed the animal smells. Cindy figured that this made sense for a wild animal. They eventually dozed off, as they both could not take being awake anymore. It was just too much

* * *

ONE CONUNDRUM IN life is that one can simply not go back. You can never go back to the way anything was, and what you remember rarely ever proves to be what was, anyway. You can only stand still or move forward. Actually, even standing still is impossible as time keeps moving forward.

Cindy was in a bit of a state. She woke up D.C. and said, "Let us make our way back to the humans. I know you have had a very, very hard time, but let us go together and see if we can make life different for you. Now that you are here, my life is different already." She had all the hope a heart can have for a small one that had been hurt. CindySleigh was determined to love him so much that he would someday be able to love her back. CindySleigh had always been a patient spirit, restless but patient. "If there is a will, there is a way," her dad would say. If Cindy had nothing else — definitely no soul left to speak of — she had determination and love. CindySleigh believed in new beginnings.

CHAPTER FIVE

Father Michael

So Cindy and D.C. started their way to Nogales, where Father Michael was at a retreat in the local Catholic church. The trip was not far, but Cindy felt a certain heaviness she had never experienced before. As they walked, D.C. would look up at her and say, "Cindy, I love you." Cindy knew D.C. did not know what those words meant, but she told him that she loved him too. The words gave voice to the fact that Cindy and D.C. were together, in every sense. She could see he was tired and picked him up, carrying him the rest of the way. D.C. fell asleep with his arms wrapped around her shoulders. Cindy cried. She had never, ever felt this before, the trusting deep weight of a sleeping child. It was a novel form of being alive.

They entered Nogales in the late morning. Cindy stopped at a store to buy clothes for the wild one. She never saw such delight in things as D.C. had. It was as though pants were love, T-shirts were love, and socks were love. All the time Cindy spent with D.C., this would never change. He truly loved her when she brought him something, anything; whether he wanted it or would ever use it was totally inconsequential. For the wild animal, things equaled love. Being raised by El Diablo until the age of six could not have been a good thing. "How he must have suffered! Can the outer glow and inner pain ever mesh in this child?" thought Cindy as D.C. glowed in his new clothes. "Will I be able to teach him to love himself? Will I be able to teach this wild animal to use a toilet? Will I be able to help him to use utensils when he eats?" There were many things to ponder as she led him by his hand to meet Father Michael. CindySleigh felt ominous times approaching. And she rarely ever missed the mark.

They pulled the thick rope, ringing the bell to beckon the priest. Father Michael walked calmly towards the Cindy he loved, who ran towards him at full speed. She threw herself into his arms. He awkwardly muttered, "Dear one, dear one, not here," but he was smiling nonetheless. Then he spied D.C. standing underneath the archway with his thumb in his mouth. "What have you brought me, CindySleigh?" There was a slight downturn in his voice, and he became very quiet.

For most of Cindy's life, Father Michael had been not just her lover but also her protector. In the chaos on earth, Cindy moved through time as if in a dream. She drifted, she absorbed, she reflected. Timetables and days of the week did not exist for her. Father Michael did not expect Cindy to move linearly in her body or in time. He lovingly took on many earthly tasks, so she could be creative and free to explore however she needed to. He allowed for her impulsiveness; her impatience; her lack of social grace; the many, many earthly tasks she resisted — dentists, doctors, taxes, phone calls, driving; and worst of all, her dread of all numbers. Cindy was not always as grateful as she should have been, for this kind of love is quietly caring and not at all like the movies. Father Michael and Cindy were the same build. They shared clothes, each loving to wear the other's. It was like wearing love. Father Michael had a passion for stealing Cindy's sweatshirts. After they made love, Cindy would wear his white V-neck T-shirt, all day, just to keep his scent close.

Cindy held Father Michael's hand, walking him over to meet D.C. D.C.'s burnt-umber eyes could bore holes into you. They seemed to look through Father Michael instead of at him. Father Michael extended his right hand, and D.C. stepped back. "D.C., do not be afraid," Cindy said. "This is how humans extend a greeting to one another." She knelt by D.C. and held his hand. Then she gently placed his hand on Father Michael's. Both the wild one and Father Michael attempted to smile, but there were more than a few shaky moments, while the two of them just stood there looking at each other, neither knowing what to say.

Father Michael, wanting to talk to Cindy alone, suggested that D.C. might benefit from a nap in one of the monk's cells. But D.C. clung to Cindy's leg and there was no way he was letting go. There was no choice but to proceed with D.C. there.

"I found him, and he has no place else to go. I thought we should keep D.C. with us," Cindy said in a casual, off-handed, insanely nervous way. "CindySleigh," Father Michael smiled, "surely you can do better than that story. I have heard and experienced many of your adventures, and nothing is ever this simple. How about some truth this time around?"

Cindy looked at the ground and sighed. She explained her "small" exchange with Mephistopheles: a soul for a child of her own. She did not look up. (In fact, she has never been able to look up and face Father Michael since that moment seven years ago.) Father Michael just stood there with his mouth wide open and his hands over his eyes. He began to cry and cry and cry. Then D.C. began to smell bad, and Cindy left Father Michael standing there alone sobbing, while she took the small wild one to the bathroom to clean up.

* * *

WHEN CINDY AND D.C. returned to where Father Michael stood, he was gone. There was an envelope with some money and a note left inside:

To the two children,

> To the one I love and the one I could perhaps love someday. Someday is not now. Now I have to separate myself to try to understand what has happened so I can

decide what I need to do. Please do not go far away, Find a place nearby. Visit me on occasion here at the church. We shall have to feel our way for now. All three of us are joined in a web that is wrapped round us fully. This space is a vacuum containing all of the shadows you have ever seen. They are seamlessly joined together in black. This is no ordinary night with stars and a half moon. This darkness is a void that cannot be spoken of, let alone described. This will take me time, Cindy. You will have to wait and see if I can be with a soulless woman and a demon's child. I know you have made your decision from a pure heart. That may just not be enough this time. Stop by later on and I will come out to be with you both if I am able.

Love,

Your Father Michael

Cindy took hold of D.C.'s hand and walked out of the chapel. The people moved away from them as they walked out on the street. All they could see was a gray fog slowly moving down the street. Cindy and D.C. were there but could not be seen. The people would cross themselves and move away.

Even in a complete fog, CindySleigh's mind never ceased to keep moving, thinking, feeling. She was weighing the loss of her soul. She was weighing the loss of her beloved. She was carrying burlap sacks filled with river rocks. There would be no swimming in the river today or for many years to come. The fog momentarily stopped as she knelt down and wrapped herself around the small wild one. He looked at her wet eyes with a certain vacancy.

〜〜 🐐

Opening up the lid,
only a slip of a lift, to see
what is
inside
the box the gods gave
to Pandora,
for her not to open,
knowing surely
she would.

Just a sliver of space
with one eye peering in.
The simple
desire
to know.

A swarm of evils
escaped.
The box contained
a vacuum
of great expanse,
creating havoc
and pain.

The balance
seems out of.

I curse the unknown
I seek.
There is no cure
for the disease
of regret.

Oh, that I could
wrap that box
with one thousand
yards of string,
twine, rope, yarn.
Anything I could find so
it would be finally
and completely encased
forever.

Even the Minotaur
could not find his way
out of the maze.
Half man, half bull,
half mad from containment
without end.

He should have been sent
Pandora, with her box
so totally entwined.
They could sit and
talk about all
that could be

outside the maze
or inside of
the box.

CHAPTER SIX

Endings are Beginnings

C indy found a small house outside of Nogales where she and D.C. could live and still be near Father Michael. Inside this bungalow the walls were old and faded, but each one was a different color: light yellow, sea green, soft turquoise, pale blue. The furniture was wood and also painted in this way, with all the colors combined on each piece and lots of the wood showing through. Cindy asked about the beautiful nature of this house. The landlord explained that sailors built it from the boats that were no longer usable. This made Cindy glow all around her edges, for she was beginning a journey, and the open sea was in their house. D.C. wanted to know where the television was, and they found a small one in the kitchen. He walked over, turned it on, and sat twelve inches in front of it, staring. Cindy gave the landlord some of Father Michael's money so he could be on his way.

She stood for an hour, watching D.C. watch T.V. He hardly ever blinked, his mouth slightly open. She asked him, "What do you see?"

He replied, "The world."

Cindy asked, "What is out there?" while holding the front door open. His eyes got very wide, and he did not respond. D.C. was very afraid. Cindy needed a plan. She knew he loved getting new things, so she suggested they go out and buy some puzzles, playing cards, and games. They could spend time together and get to know each other better. At the thought of shopping, he jumped up and ran to her. "First, you have to clean up and wash your hands," Cindy said.

He pleaded, "Come with me, please." She complied, and he insisted they leave the door open while she cleaned him up. All the doors were left open from that time on, so D.C. would not feel closed in.

They left, hand in hand, for the marketplace of Nogales, to get toys, puzzles, and all the things that children love to play with and need to grow. With that task completed, she took him to the booth of Faustino to begin her real mission. Faustino and Cindy hugged upon seeing each other, feeling close in their knowing. Cindy asked D.C. to look around the booth for things that reminded him of his past. Objects took on a different form in this booth. Cindy had a suspicion that Faustino shaped them for each person who walked in. While D.C. was searching, Cindy found a green wooden box with hinges that was very old. "Hey, D.C. we can put things in here." It turned out green was D.C.'s favorite color. Cindy put the box on the ground, open, in the middle of the booth.

D.C. brought Cindy a candle and a key. "Can you tie them together before you put them in?" he asked.

"Sure, honey, but what does it mean?" replied Cindy.

"Locked in a dark closet," he responded. Faustino gave Cindy some string, and she tied the candle and key together and put them in the box. After hearing DC's confession, Faustino and Cindy watched the small wild one become very agitated. He stood on his tiptoes, rocking to and fro, moving his hands as if his fingers were telling a story. In a trancelike state, he mouthed some other type of language. Then he stopped. He eyed a tiny crib and brought it to Cindy. "Not allowed out." It looked like a jail cell to CindySleigh. Every step forward, brought her one step further into a strange sadness.

D.C. shouted with glee when he found a small metal piece Faustino had fashioned to look like a television. "Space," he announced. Then D.C. found a pile of Faustino's rubber bands and proceeded to make a ball out of them, about three inches in diameter. When he brought the ball to Cindy, he simply said, "Inside." Later on D.C. found a beautifully carved wooden heart, hand-painted red. To Cindy's surprise, he took Faustino's hammer and smashed the heart. She silently picked up all the pieces and placed them inside the box. The rocking on tiptoes and speaking in tongues had begun again.

Cindy watched and waited. If she was to help D.C., she had to know how he saw the world. This trip had provided the clues she still had to work out. Finally D.C. came out of his trance and sat down next to Cindy. Together, they looked inside the box.

"The darkness you lived in will be sealed inside this box when we close it, D.C. If there is anything else that you want to put in, now is the time," said Cindy.

D.C. put all of his fingertips in the box and stared into it with his burnt-umber eyes. Cindy saw smoke sifting out from under its lid. Afterwards D.C hopped up and ran away. When Cindy looked inside the box, there were burn marks where he had made his pain visible.

She turned to the shopkeeper and said, "Thank you, Faustino, for your patience and help."

"Señora, I will do all I can to help you."

"In that case, I need all the string, twine, rope, and yarn you have. I need to assure myself that these evils do not ever escape." So, as D.C. played nearby with the many things in Faustino's booth, Cindy sat and wrapped and wrapped and wrapped. Faustino muttered in tongues a bit himself as he watched Cindy intently using her most potent magic to try to help create a new life for D.C. She was closing up the darkness. CindySleigh was wrapping it in, so it would stay in the box, forever in the past, never ever to see the light of day.

CHAPTER SEVEN

The Boathouse

Cindy and D.C. began daily life in the bungalow of boats. During the day, Cindy would try to teach D.C. the ways to be human. She sent him off to school with peanut butter and jelly sandwiches, comforted his restless nights, and held his hand. These things were so precious to her. She never thought in this life she would ever have a chance to be a mother and would hold her child's hand as they crossed the street. She would beam with joy. D.C. was so charming in the outside world. Despite his charm, people watched this odd pair, knowing there was something different about them. Sometimes they would step aside and whisper. Cindy ignored the murmurs as she always did. She lived with goodness in her heart, and that was enough for her. They would be with Father Michael whenever he was able. Cindy would watch D.C. and Father Michael walk down the street using the exact same gait. It was wonderful.

The other side of wonderful was that D.C. was still feral. No matter how many different ways Cindy tried to help him and teach him, nothing she tried ever really worked. Inside, she insisted D.C. was a normal small boy. She could delude herself for quite a long time, but it was not true. D.C. would keep his animal self hidden in public, but sometimes in the house of colors, Black would reappear. He would howl and nip and bite Cindy, cornering her with wild, bare-toothed growls. Black knew how much Cindy loved D.C. and wanted him to grow. Black would kick this vulnerability around like a ball. He would lie on her lap as D.C. She would hold him and hug him and sing to him. Suddenly his curls would turn into fur. Black would appear and eye her with the same burnt-umber eyes. He would snarl, curl up his lip, turn on her, and attack.

Afterwards, while applying alcohol to the scratches and teeth marks from his many bites, Cindy would sit and cry. She cried from the pain of the wounds, but mostly she cried because she loved him so and could not keep his darkness in the box of one thousand strings. Cindy would become lost inside after D.C.'s rampages. This world was now her only world. Black would come over to lick her wounds with his tongue, snuggling in next to her. And Cindy would pet him, knowing he knew no other way. Then he would jump up and run to his bed, leaping in to circle round, before settling into a deep sleep. Cindy would take a really hot bath, then smoke a cigarette in a daze. The house would begin to groan like a ship, tied to moorings, that needed to set sail. It moaned and scraped and sighed for all that was going on inside its painted walls.

After one of these many nights, while Cindy was smoking at the window, Mephistopheles appeared. "So, how's it going, mamacita?" Normally, CindySleigh would have punched him with a jab to the stomach, followed by a fast kick to the exact same spot. Hurting so much from her endless wounds, Cindy, at first, did not respond. Her spirit and body had become emaciated over time. She did not even bother to protect herself when Black attacked.

"You seem pleased," she finally managed to respond.

"I did not create this desire, CindySleigh. You invented this all on your own, and with fervor, I might add. It is easy to blame me for your longings. The truth is, your wish has been granted, and longings never take you where you expect." El Diablo was not gloating.

Cindy thought about how she had made the conscious choice that created her current reality. "Where is the path of change I cannot see?" she asked.

"You now speak in the realm of humanness. I have no answers for your world. I live in the realm of the unknown," Mephistopheles replied. He did not seem evil to CindySleigh, right then but rather part of the makeup of the unseen and the unexplained that was her life.

This was all too hard, so CindySleigh decided to go to bed. Cindy lay awake feeling paralyzed. The bungalow of boats began to moan, scrape, and groan as it never had before. The house pulled and cut at the ropes that held it at bay. Cindy's bed began to jerk and sway. Objects flew all over the room. She kept hearing the sounds of breaking glass. Then the table and the chairs fell, crashing. She could hear them drag across what used to be a wall. The bungalow had lost its moorings. The rocking of this *now-boat* house was terrifying. The ground shifted beneath her feet from to side to side: floor became ceiling, ceiling became wall, wall became floor.

Cindy pulled herself down to a window and saw a tumultuous, acid-green, black sea. She found herself in the Author's dream of the boca de cielo. Cindy was numb and motionless in this ocean. The water slammed against the walls of her bedroom. She was soaked to the skin, glowing phosphorescent green in the dark of midnight. Even in this state, she was desperately worried about D.C. She began to crawl to his bedroom, just as he left it, trying to make his way to her. When they found each other, he clung to her with both his arms and legs. She kept running her hands through the curls on his head, murmuring the countless nothing words that keep beings alive when they are at the mouth of heaven and it appears to be hell.

CHAPTER EIGHT

The Storm

The house began to split apart in the storm, broken apart by huge smashing waves. A wave would slap Cindy's entire body and throw her on her back before she saw it coming. Another would follow before she could catch her breath. D.C. and Cindy held on to each other the best that they could, but the waves would fling them apart. The thunder was deafening. The darkness seemed eternal except for occasional seconds of lightning flashing too much light, making hot, sizzling, cracking sounds as it hit the water near them. Cindy began to yell at D.C., "If we get separated, you must swim to shore. You know how to swim. You must swim. When the lightning strikes, you will see the white of the beach. I know you can make it."

As he took in Cindy's instructions, D.C. saw a candescent vein of brilliant lightning strike her. All turned dark and she disappeared. The next bolt struck much farther away, and he could see the light white of the shore. D.C. used all his muscle, breath, and spirit to do what his mother had told him to do. He began to swim, never losing sight of the beach when the lightning flashed. He would dive through the giant dark waves and then continue kicking his feet. He swam, never losing sight of his goal — his life.

Cindy was sinking. She slid and was bent by the dictates of the black all around her. Nothing, however, could stop the mind of CindySleigh from working. "I am a lizard," Cindy said to herself. "I could not hold onto him. I pushed him away from me. My heart is cold, my blood is ice. I am a cold-blooded animal."

She plunged farther down into the water, for it suddenly felt like home. It was deep and black, like the void Cindy had inside where her organs used to be. She began swimming down with her eyes wide open.

When she looked at her hands, lizard-like claws began to appear. All around her and all inside her was black. Between the water and Cindy, there was only the thin layer of skin, with green scales growing upon it. She was becoming transparent. She saw nothing and felt nothing but black. She surrendered to the blackness of the sea, surrendered to her claws and admired them.

Cindy was dying in the slow motion of fluid movement. Blackness was inside, all around, so complete. She ceased needing air. Life was so confusing on the surface. She saw all the textures and colors. She was acutely aware of all the chaos of living. This was so much easier, and she leisurely swam downward, wandering deep underwater, letting the void comfort her cold heart in a way no human person ever could.

All of a sudden, her head came up through the surface

of the water, water slick like glass. She had arrived within a cave. Its surface was dark, shining chunks of rock. There was a dim light, but Cindy could not see the source. Across the water, a three-headed dog howled at her, and a hooded being glowered with his non-human face. CindySleigh had cheated Charon of his coin. The rules of death were not usually broken in this way. Cindy decided quickly that she should swim downstream, to get away from these creatures. She swam to the opposite bank and using her lizard claws climbed slowly onto its obliquely shining surface. Cindy pulled herself up. She lay there, her right ear placed down on the cold, dark rock, and became comatose. No dreams, no thoughts, only blank, black spaces in front of her.

WHEN SHE AWOKE she was in a forest filled with maple, beech, and evergreen trees. She walked on through meadows filled with Queen Anne's lace and clover. Cindy occasionally glanced down to look for one with four leaves. Luck eluded her. When her arms were crossed she could see through them. "Interesting," she thought. The sunlight in which she walked did not warm her skin. Cindy realized this world was like a drawing, a beautiful drawing. The trees, grass, and sky had been drawn on a piece of paper you could just rip into two. Cindy looked through both of her hands down to her feet and realized she was dead.

* * *

THE AUTHOR AND Mephistopheles stood under the gazebo watching the storm. It held their attention — almost without breath — with the havoc it wreaked. The wind was fierce, and the clouds billowed gray, black, and dark lavender with an occasional flash of whiter-than-white lightning, making spiderwebs from opposite edges of the sky, before it would sear down to meet the boca de cielo and crack into the sea. Smoke would rise from the point where it hit, spiraling up to the sky until the next crack would sound. Smoke and fire were arguing with the mouth of heaven. The thunder that followed shook the ground on which the two onlookers stood. It made the sands of the shore quiver and move in myriad patterns as if each and every grain of sand wanted to escape from this place.

Lightning struck again. This time it made its mark in the sand near them. Sand flew straight up as melting silicon from the deep hole. It stayed frozen in that erupted shape as glass. The rain came down as sheets of water. It spit and hissed as it hit the freshly made glass vortex. Giant raindrops enmeshed the sky and the sea until they became one.

The Author and Mephistopheles were on a small island of earth surrounded by the tumult of decisions being interrupted. The future was being reinvented by emotion. It made all they saw seem wavy, as if the world all around them turned into visual moiré patterns. No longer at odds with each other, El Diablo and the Author stood together, both moving their lips, murmuring. The soft sounds they uttered, attempting to use the secret power of half-spoken words to calm this storm, were to no avail.

Carried by the waves of emotion, the floating remains of a house appeared and disappeared with the flashes of lightning. The pair hauled up a section of wooden porch, grabbing its banister so tightly that their knuckles blanched white, and climbed aboard. From the vantage of the porch, they desperately tried to see the future that was being shaped, but nothing they witnessed gave them clarity.

Time began to stretch as they saw the strongest line from the veins of blinding light slowly move down from the heavens and split apart the last of the floating house before it sank. Pieces of wood exploded. Yellow, blue, green lengths of lumber, each burning like giant matches, flying slow motion into the sky until gravity pulled them back into time, extinguishing them in the sea.

Smoke billowed from this last strike, springing up like a leaping deer as lightning hit the water. The smoke itself was flesh-colored and danced its way upward to the sky, fusing the color of blood with the deep lavenders and grays of the clouds. The thunder that followed echoed from the grave.

The Author immediately knew some very important part of her was quite simply no more. She dropped her head, knowing the numbness of loss, feeling it move through every cell. This loss cannot be found; this loss cannot be replaced. When you feel this non-feeling, your body takes on a surreal lightness. That is the numb. Yet, there also is a deep heaviness that gives all movement the sensation of stretching limbs through earth rather than air.

The Author's weight was as stone. She began walking in circles on the salvaged remains of the wooden porch. She walked so long that she wore a deep trench into the wood. She walked and walked on the same path that led her always back to where she began, knowing that no one can begin again.

CHAPTER NINE

Netherworld

I t was amazing how quickly the storm subsided, leaving a calm, mysterious sea. The full moon dimly lit the evening's passage, as the Author eyed a small shape on the sand. Both she and El Diablo started to run — it was D.C. on the shore.

THE AUTHOR ROLLED him onto his back. D.C.'s skin was gray-green in color. She put her ear close to his lips and her hand on his heart, anxiously waiting for sounds of life.

"Do something, you idiot!" Mephistopheles screamed.

The Author turned to him, with ice in her eyes, and calmly said, "You, the Iago of demons, led me into this mess and now have the nerve to scream at me? I thought this would be the icing on the primordial cake for you. Now, you have two souls for the price of one." She solemnly turned back to D.C., moved her arm in a full circle before pounding his chest. Then she placed her ear to his heart and listened, hoping for a tremor. Nothing.

Mephistopheles began to howl. His animal sound echoing, in the dark of the night, throughout the air of the boca de cielo. The echo became a round of his continuous cries bellowing into the night.

The Author was confused. "El Diablo, will you shut up and calm down. What exactly is your problem?

Tears emerged from his eyes and then flew off his face as if attempting to escape his darkness. "Black, my Black for all eternity. What do you, stupid humans, bumbling about for seconds, know about eternal, unconditional love? Nothing. My one and only, my familiar is in there," pointing to the small child, "and dying, too."

The Author seized this unusual opportunity. Leverage with the Devil does not often present itself. She had to think quickly because her bargaining chip was D.C., and he was dying. The Author jumped to her feet. "What will you give me if I can bring them back?" Her mind raced all over the place. "Never mind that question. Where is CindySleigh?" the Author asked, stumbling over her own words.

"She is in the Elysian Fields, the shadow world," El Diablo replied.

"Fine." The Author's mind had begun to focus. There was no time for confusion. She took a deep breath, doing her best to remain calm, trying to think quickly and clearly. Then she played her best hand. "Here's the deal. You get Cindy up on the surface, and I will do mouth-to-mouth resuscitation, as only a human can. If Black and D.C. live, they live with me. I'll take my chances with them, even though I know they might kill Cindy if you don't first."

The Devil did not have eternity on his side, either. He

had to decide now. He looked at her and nodded. They gathered their hands together and made a silent pact.

Then the Author spun around, immediately setting to the task of reviving D.C. As she pounded on D.C.'s chest, he would change periodically from small child to the black wild dog. She waited until the human form appeared, then held his nose and did the regularly paced breathing repetitions, in and out, in and out, over and over again. Mephistopheles stood silently by, waiting to see if she could breathe life into these two spirits, or if they were truly gone.

Suddenly, D.C.'s form threw up sea water, and he began coughing up his own storm. The Author held him as he shape-shifted from child to animal and back to child again. Just seeing Black momentarily appear made El Diablo fold his arms and smile broadly. The Author took off her jacket and wrapped it around D.C. He looked up at her and said, "Hi, Mom," seeing only CindySleigh when he looked at the Author. She realized that D.C. had already become her child. El Diablo was quick to deliver on at least one part of the bargain. The Author smiled. She held D.C. in her arms and rocked him quietly while the two of them sat in the wet sand. El Diablo, of course, was standing nearby, watching.

THE AUTHOR ROCKED D.C. to sleep in her jacket. She was so full of love as she watched him sleep. Mephistopheles let out a silent whistle from behind her. The Author did not hear it, but Black did. In seconds, the sleeping child was a very happy wild Australian Dog, jumping in the surf chasing fish. He finally caught a rainbow trout and brought it to his master. "Put that fish back in the sea this instant, you mangy dog," the Author commanded. Black looked at El Diablo, then back at the Author, then back at El Diablo again.

"Let him eat it. Black is starving and later you won't have to feed D.C.," the Devil stated. The fish, flashing prismatic colors, wriggled for mercy out of each side of the wild dog's mouth. The Author, after much hesitation, complied with the Devil's request. Cindy would not have approved, but, then, the Author and Cindy were different creatures. As Black tore into the fish, Mephistopheles seemed to be humming a quiet melody. The Author was anxious to get down to the business of getting Cindy back. Does the Devil always keep his bargains? She did not know. Now that he had his familiar back, there was no reason he had to. Morals were not his forte.

PREPARING FOR BATTLE, the Author moved into a front stance fighting position. She was soon distracted by snow. Snow fell all around them. There was the silence and stillness of time stopping. All was hushed except for the whispered, soft melodies of Mephistopheles. Then he began to draw in the snow. He drew the patterns of two long capes. He began to whisper instructions to the Author. She shifted to an at-ease position, concentrating all her attention within her ears.

"These blankets of snow will be all the disguise you will need to get past Charon and Cerberus. This cape will fit over you and make your temperature drop, so they will not know you are alive. There is one for you and one for CindySleigh. When she comes within a certain proximity to you, her temperature will begin to rise, so Cindy will also need a cape," Mephistopheles instructed.

He walked over to a small plant, the honesty bush or money tree, and picked off some change. He rubbed them between his fingers until the outer layers came off, leaving translucent centers. He counted out nine and handed them to the Author. There were three to get the Author in, and six to get the Author and CindySleigh out. If they succeeded in bribing Charon, the Author and CindySleigh might perhaps cheat death. As he placed the milky-white seeds in the Author's hands, they turned into copper coins.

The Author knew enough not to interrupt Mephistopheles with questions and words. She was silent and very attentive. Each instruction and the order of each instruction were part of the very air of magic that surrounded her. Her task was daunting, but her love was stronger than her fear of failure.

Mephistopheles waited as she held the coins in her hands, noticing how she was ever so careful not to drop them. He waited until her heart calmed and she chose to look up at his eyes, her's filled with shadows of the unknown. "There is a cave nearby; I will take you there. At the end of the long, winding passageway, you will see a cloaked figure by the river. Hand him the three coins and let the dog smell your hand. Cerberus should catch the scent of Black on you and allow you to pass. If not, you will lose more than the hand you put near him. This is all a gamble. To trick the fates is not an easy task. Even if you succeed, as with all endeavors, sacrifices will be inevitable," Mephistopheles warned.

Mephistopheles stood very still. He demanded the Author's utmost attention. Concentration hovered within her, while time seemed randomly strewn about in an odd way that had its own order. He walked over to the drawings, lifted up one cape of snow, and placed it upon the Author's back. Then he lifted the hood and pulled it over her head until her face was completely hidden from view. Then he repeated the process with the second cape. "This one is for CindySleigh. You will find her in the Elysian Fields. She can never, and I mean *never*, see you. She will hear the sound of your voice, so you can instruct her in the way to come back to the world of the living, but she cannot see you." He looked at her with the frankness of a spirit that gives you what you want but then exacts his price when least expected.

The Author did not know if she might ever *see* CindySleigh again. How would she find her without using her eyes? If she used her eyes, Cindy might, very possibly, look back at the Author, and all would be lost.

The Author thought very hard about the deal she had struck with El Diablo. He said he would help her bring Cindy back to the surface, but he never promised that the Author would see her again. Fury gripped her stomach. This demon always saw what humans could not: the flaws in all of humanity's well-made plans, the realities humans could not predict, and always, the consequences of human actions. The Author had to use tremendous effort to hold her fighting body still, to hold her tongue still, to keep her spirit in check. This was the condition the Author had to accept if she was ever to have the presence of CindySleigh near her again. She had no choice but to proceed.

Mephistopheles watched the Author's silent yet palpable struggle, while they stood still, and the hours passed. He collected all the unseen energy needed to create a safe space where the Author could comprehend every detail. He needed to wait until her emotions separated themselves from her task. Charon could sense the feelings of the living as well as their temperature. The Devil knew the Author well; her emotions might put her mission in jeopardy. He waited until her anger subsided, her fear subsided, her longing subsided, and her self subsided.

When she was an empty cup, waiting to be filled, Mephistopheles knew it was time.

CHAPTER TEN

The Journey

Mephistopheles and the Author walked southward in silence, while the wind whistled past their ears, making quiet, mournful sounds. Black, blessedly oblivious to any future, ran circles around them, jumping straight up into the air to lick the Devil's face. El Diablo had to laugh, which made the Author laugh, encouraging Black to continue with his antics. The Author spotted the opening of the cave, which stood hardly any taller than she did, and her mood darkened. Sunlight could not penetrate its darkness. The Author called Black to her and hugged him, smoothing his fur. El Diablo promised Black would be transformed to D.C. by the time she returned, that D.C. would wait for her at the cave opening. She looked into Mephistopheles' eyes and held their gaze. Then she turned away and walked into the cave. One step into the dark and the Author disappeared.

THE AUTHOR STOOD just inside the opening and tried to peer in. It was a void. "How am I going to do this without using my eyes?" she asked herself. Panic set in. She slowly moved her right foot forward and came to an edge. "Ah, a step," she smiled to herself. The Author sat down on the step and felt all around her with her hands. The surface was much like the material of Mephistopheles' boots, smooth like glass. The edge of the stair was sharp. The Author was sure this cave was carved out of obsidian. The walls, the ceiling, and the stairs were all made out of black, volcanic, glass-like rock.

She stood up and began to walk carefully down the stairs. The Author counted the steps as she traveled downward in a slow spiral. After fifteen steps, she came to a platform and could almost see some hint of reflected dark-blue light on the walls and ceiling. Continuing down, she counted from fifteen to one over and over again; as when one falls asleep before dreaming. The steps were endless. She began to fall. Reaching out to the sides with both hands up, the Author slapped the walls, trying to stop her reckless decline. With each effort, she could feel a slice of pain.

The Author lost track of how many flights she fell. She finally came to a halt on a landing, breathing heavily. She sensed steam coming from her lips, and her body was wet from sweat. She knew she was close to her destination. Her hands were in pain. She could not see them. She lifted a palm to her lips and licked it. Blood. This would not do. Blood oozing and dripping from her hands would be an *un*dead giveaway to Charon, despite her cloak of snow. The Author pushed her hands together as hard as she could to stop the flow. "I have to figure out what to do." She stared straight into the humid black of nothing, letting the blank in.

She lifted Cindy's cloak off of her back. The snow was fresh and light. It did not seem to be affected by the heat and humidity. The Author used Cindy's cloak to wipe the blood from her hands and her mouth, knowing that she would need to, then, leave it behind. To keep the unknown at bay, the Author sat and began to eat the snow from Cindy's cloak. There was nothing like the taste of freshly fallen snow. It calmed more than her thirst.

She continued down towards the heat and the glowing dark-blue light. The Author was going to find CindySleigh. She heard the sound of water, and she knew the river Styx would be at the next turn. The Author pulled her cloak as far as she could over her face and wrapped it across her front to cover the rest of her body. She hoped but could not know if the bleeding had stopped.

The Author felt for the edge of the next step with her right foot, but there was no edge as far as she could feel. She walked forward, and the blue light reflected darkly all around her. To her left, the Author spied the three-headed dog. He watched her with all six of his eyes while his throats let out low, raspy growls. Next to Cerberus stood his master, Charon. Charon wore a robe caked with mud and his body was covered with the filth of many centuries. He did not really look at the Author but rather glanced in her direction as if he was blind and had heard her step.

The river seemed more like hot sludge than water, slowly moving past. Steam was rising, thick like fog, from the river Styx, allowing for no real vision, no real sight. The fog would part as the Author walked forward. She reached deep into her pockets for the coins. As she came near Cerberus, he bared his teeth, looking ready for the kill. Charon seemed totally unaware of her presence.

There was no way in hell that the Author was putting her potentially bloody hand near three growling mouths! She turned and slipped into the river, cursing the entire time. Charon repeatedly damned her to eternal hell, even if it meant killing the Author himself. The Author just kept treading mud, moving towards hell without the help of any curses. Charon got in his boat in an attempt to catch her, but she was already climbing out of the river on the other side. Coated with mud, the Author ran fiercely through halls of black obsidian. She tripped, fell, and hit her head, inviting even deeper blackness.

* * *

WHEN SHE AWOKE, the Author found herself in the Elysian Fields. The drawing contained no color for her eyes. "How should I begin my search for Cindy? If I were Cindy, where would I be?" she mused aloud. Not one part of this expedition had gone according to plan, and how could she sense the flow of movement in a land without life? The mud caked on her skin, and she looked like a woman made of clay as she moved though the gray-and-white trees of this underworld. Gray people moved past her, but their movements made no sound. She picked a few stalks of Queen Anne's lace from the field. Her hands did not feel the stems or any resistance upon breaking them. The flowers did not smell, and her ears were ringing with sharp sounds that blocked out the continuous silence.

The Author turned completely around three times. After three cycles of seeking, she began to hear a trickling sound from up ahead. She ran towards it as fast as she could, feeling like someone had suddenly lit a match to guide her, in the darkest of nights. Her running had no sound, so the water's forever-changing sounds were easy to track.

There was a small creek over to the left. CindySleigh was sitting cross-legged at the edge, watching the water, her back to the Author. CindySleigh and the Author had both sought out the only sign of life among the dead: moving water. Moving water speaks if one listens closely. It tells the stories of all time and each moment, all at once. It burbles and shushes; it slides and it sings.

The river told Cindy that the Author was behind her. The Author mouthed, "Do not, for any reason, turn and look at me." Cindy could hear the Author without sound.

Cindy responded, "I am not dead, as I have many souls. I am less one. A big one, but one is not all I am or can be. I still have anima. I still can go up to the surface. I have not because I have unwittingly hurt a small boy that I love very much. Our short time together was so strong and intense, but in the end I failed him and myself. What has passed can never be repaired. I am better in the gray world of the unliving and unloving. I do not think I can bear the pain of seeing D.C. again. The river has been telling me stories of others. Stories of their successes and failures, wishes and dreams, their fears and sadness. I cannot go back with you. I am one of these stories you write and the river sings."

The Author listened carefully to Cindy's silent words. She did not reply. Sadness hung around the two of them. Cindy mouthed to the Author, "Close your eyes and lift up your hands in front of you at shoulder width." The Author complied. CindySleigh rose up and could see from where she stood the black lines left from the slashes on the palms of the Author's hands. "This pain, this story, and this burden I can take away from you." Cindy walked to the Author and placed her palms on the Author's palms. Cindy closed her eyes. They stood there, trembling and touching. Then Cindy pulled her hands back. Her hands resisted, as if pulling from a vacuum. Cindy walked back to the river and sat down, cross-legged, facing away from the Author. She viewed the slashes in her palms in a thoughtful way. The Author lowered her own hands and looked at her own palms; the cuts, blood, and scars were gone.

THE AUTHOR TOLD Cindy that she would take care of D.C. as best she could. Cindy wept with no tears; the river made the sound of crying people, and the water leapt up to create rivulets that ran down her face. "Thank you, Author. Perhaps we will meet on the surface again someday. The river is a comfort to me until then."

The Author gazed at CindySleigh for a long, loving time before she turned around to find her way back to the cave. The Author had run out of words. There were no words that could comfort CindySleigh. Only Cindy could take herself out of hell. With that thought fresh in her brain, the Author turned and walked away.

CHAPTER ELEVEN

The Garden

Cindy sat and waited. Cindy sat and stared at the cuts on her hands and smiled. "I have removed these from the Author. She took on what I could not. She does not need to carry the scars of my folly." The river murmured reassurances to CindySleigh. Cindy unfocused her eyes, letting them rest upon the river. The sun scattered its light across the surface of the water, making small sparks of fire. The glittering points of light moved like flocks of small birds swarming about in the sky. CindySleigh received, received, and received. She knew that apparent change could be made in a day, a week, a month. Real transformation is a daily arduous task that has to be tended to like a garden one loves.

Cindy dipped her hands in the water. It caressed the wounds on her palms, easing the pain. She was not the least bit concerned. These cuts will turn into scars, a visual reminder of her encounter with Mephistopheles. A reminder of where love and longing can take you, especially when spirited up from El Diablo. Cindy had no regrets as she sat, letting the river swirl all around her hands. The sun of light but not heat passed from one side of the drawing to the other side of the page many times. The moon traveled through all of its sequential phases. Cindy would note them each night as she was being healed by the whispering melodies the river invented just for her. The water, always changing, gently caressed her emotions. Gradually the black lines across her palms became pink with new skin. Grasses and wildflowers sprang up around her as she sat so still, cross-legged by the edge of the water. Time passed in an unending symphonic movement. The wind, sun, clouds, trees, grasses, rippling streams all added their part, singing harmonies in time.

Cindy noticed cornflowers blooming next to her chin. They kept the company of daisies and, of course, Queen Anne's lace, which to Cindy was like a flurry of snowflakes in the heart of the summer. She stood up and began gathering all the stones she could find to create a partial dam in the river. Cindy did not want to stop the flow of the water, she only wanted to give it a short detour, which she dug with her hands. It was a winding maze with twists and bends that always returned eventually to the source of the stream. When finished, she rinsed her hands in the river and began to walk. It felt good to move after sitting for so long.

CINDY WALKED RANDOMLY through the Elysian Fields, searching for the first plant to put in her garden. It was a plant of the past that would only bloom in the tenderest conditions of the spring; folding down and quitting by July: the Bleeding Heart. There it was with its many white centers encircled with pink, hanging so gracefully from the bending stems of the bush. Cindy dug wide so as not to lose any of the roots and carried it back to the maze by the river. She planted it in the morning side of the garden, on the far left to begin her spiral. She almost sat down to listen to another of the river's stories. They were so rich and tempting, but she realized she needed morning glories and went back out in search of the heavenly blues for healing.

As she walked, Cindy noticed that the sun was past peak, and she understood why they were hiding. She would have to wait until morning when they opened up in their daily way with the rising sun. Instead, Cindy found countless ferns that mimicked the spiral of her garden as they grew. She took as many as her two arms could carry, adding magic and sincerity to the garden. She dug well into the evening and fell asleep with much soil on her hands.

WHEN SHE AWOKE, the heavenly blue morning glories were only yards away, and she planted them near the pink dogwood tree. Cindy wound grapevines up through the branches so the heavenly blues could cling and climb. All morning, CindySleigh collected the mourning of the past in flowers. "I change but in death," the bay leaf told her as she carefully lifted it up with all its roots intact. Periwinkles reminded her of the pleasures of memory and prompted her to think about absent friends and family. So much love missed and held close at the same time. Cindy planted a sweetbrier bush to heal her wounds. These were the flowers of the past that resided in the morning garden of CindySleigh.

The sun was high, and Cindy felt warmth inside as she tasted her peppermint. She put in thyme for courage and ginger for the strength she needed for the second half of the day. She recalled how daisy actually means, "the day's eye." They open and close with the sun. Transplanting daisies to a cultivated garden is considered very unlucky, so luckily for CindySleigh they were already in place with their white petals reaching up to the light. She walked through the fields searching for the meaning of midday in her heart. She found calendulas. Their fringed orange petals would follow the sunlight from left to right in this drawing of nature. Cindy put narcissus by the river so they could admire their reflection in the water and be at peace.

Then on her second walk, as she scoured the underworld, Cindy found five red hibiscus which she planted in a ring near the center. "We are consumed by love," they whispered to CindySleigh. Cindy began to move the dirt very carefully until she uncovered the remains of a doe, peacefully at rest on her side. Cindy, with reverence for what was, covered the quiet remains, then planted grass, so the site would not be disturbed. She glanced in the river and noticed that her skin had turned a light green. She liked the way her pink scars glowed against the green.

Exhausted by her efforts, Cindy lay on the grass which she now matched. She was filthy, from head to toe, after trying to create some sort of order. She could not sleep. She watched the full moon rise. The air was suddenly full of wonderful smells. Following her nose, Cindy walked through the silver light of the moon and found night-flowering jasmine. So sensual and heady was the smell, Cindy had to sit for a while before beginning the garden of sleep.

Hours were spent moving in slow motion that night as Cindy blindly searched for her evening-garden flowers. Perhaps it was the poppies that made her feel like a somnambulist in her task. Her sense of smell acute, she moved through air as though it were water. The poppies reminded Cindy that she was in oblivion, but she did not mind. She pricked herself with bittersweet. She sucked the blood until it stopped bleeding, noticing it, too, was green. She went straight to the open white trumpets of the moonflowers that bloom only by the soft light of dark. At night, when the nose becomes the eye, the heart and the head meld. Cindy snuggled next to the poppies, and in her dreams, all the days she lived combined into one day.

WHEN CINDY WOKE up and yawned, flower seeds spilled

out of her mouth. She looked at her hands and feet to find the beginning of roots growing from her fingers and toes. For a while, Cindy held her breath. She was becoming inseparable from the garden. CindySleigh did not want this to happen. Upon her exhale, flowers flowed out of her mouth. Growing color abounded and saturated her eyes with the glory of what is. Her being was telling Cindy if she did not leave now, she would not leave at all. Cindy looked upon the garden of her life, and it was good. She was ready to depart from this halfway place. CindySleigh was ready to live.

Her decision grew like the roots in her garden, underneath the earth in this underworld place of half-lives. As she created sorrow and joy in the beauty of the flowers, her breath expanded and her head became an open grassy field that saw no end.

She jumped into the river and swam upstream. Cindy's upper body strength was more than ready for the journey. The digging and planting, all her passion for color, beauty, and the truth of her garden gave her new-found strength. Her arms were mighty machines moving in and through the water: The water made way for CindySleigh. She slid through with no thought of outcome. At some point of no consciousness, Cindy cut through the drawing of the Elysian Fields and swam out in the open sea. Her only direction was forward, and forward she swam. When Cindy experienced any doubt, she heard the voice of Sir saying clearly, "We become better by doing that which we cannot do," and she swam on.

The water was gray and tasted of salt. The sky mirrored its metallic dullness. Cindy looked to her right and thought, "Is this Emerald City? How can it be, for it is steel gray?" She suddenly gasped and grasped where she was. Cindy saw Manhattan to her right; she used all of her fortitude to swim up the Hudson River towards home. She took a moment to tread water. CindySleigh was filled with rapture and yelled out loudly, throwing her fist up in the air.

A SMALL BLACK rowboat silently appeared on her left. Waving from the boat was was Mephistopheles. Cindy was in no mood for him. She would offer him no words. "Cin, climb into the boat," he demanded, countless times. Cindy stayed in the water and stared at him. No words come from her mouth. "Cindy, you will freeze to death if you do not get into the boat. Does that not seem stupid after all you have been through?" Mephistopheles sounded sincere, but then the trouble that appears is never in what he says but rather in what he leaves out of his sentences.

"At what cost, specifically?" Cindy replied, adding, "Leave no stone unturned, for my fist of stone will pummel you senseless if you should bring me or anyone I love in harm's way."

Mephistopheles looked at her and let out a sigh filled with weariness. "Come into the boat. You are freezing to death. The debt has been paid. Come into the boat."

Cindy was firm, "I want specifics, and I want them without ambiguity, or I will go back to the underworld and grow into the garden I know awaits me someday. Today could be that day. I would rather physically die than suffer the death of my spirit ever again. On this, I am perfectly clear."

Mephistopheles closed his eyes, as if revealing his heart caused him much pain. "The Author saved Black from death. You see, I, too, know of love. I swore I would help you resurface alive on earth, and here I am, so will you please, please get in the boat? It was an exchange. There is no debt. Your lips are deep plum, and there is not much time left."

CindySleigh could sense in and around her solar plexus that what he said was true. Mephistopheles reached into the water, put his arms around her, and the next thing Cindy knew, she was sitting in his black rowboat, shivering uncontrollably. "Here, put this around you so you can gather the warmth you need." Mephistopheles covered Cindy with a beautiful, huge wolf pelt. It was gray and white, and Cindy sat quietly, absorbed in its texture. She sat and stroked the soft fur over and over again. She examined the head filled with teeth and the holes where the animal's eyes once were. She held the remains of the wolf's paws and had waking dreams of running wild through the woods. Suddenly, Cindy was back in the rowboat. "May I keep this pelt?" she asked El Diablo.

"It has always been yours," he replied. Her shivering ceased. CindySleigh sat calmly and listened. She heard the sound of the oars as Mephistopheles dipped them into the water repeatedly, pulling them slowly back to shore.

Plate twelve "the Black Dog of Marblestown"   Artist signature

BLANK

C indy became aware of the sound of a man's voice hollering. From the smell of wet, rotting leaves, she knew the time of year. It was late fall. Her arms and legs shivered from dampness. Her white T-shirt and jeans were wet from the soft steady rain. Mist floated up from the ground as if from the dry ice of a stage production. The rain dripped down her face. Her clothes stuck to her body.

As she raised her arms to hug herself, she heard the clank of metal hitting metal and saw her wrists bound with silver chains. She held her hands up to the sky as if to question, but no answer came. The metal clinked as she lowered her arms. Then she saw her bare feet, also bound in chains. In the immediate distance, she could see nothing through the rain, only hear the crush of people and their voices. One voice in particular rang out clearly.

"What price? What price will you pay for this strong, older woman? What price for what looks frail but could be full of spirit and sprightly? What price will you pay for unknown possibility? She'll give you a run for your money, this one. What do I hear? Let the bidding begin."

Cindy searched her memory. Where was her life? What was her life? She held her head in her chained hands, knowing she was being auctioned off, but that was now.

What had happened to then? Her mind was swept clean like the inside of an all-white room. Silent, peaceful, blank ... all memory erased. She longed for a mirror. Perhaps seeing her face would give her a clue as to who she was. Cindy thought she must have worn glasses. Her view, filled with leaves floating down amid the raindrops, looked slightly out of focus. Without memory, without emotion, CindySleigh stood on the slaves' block waiting ... waiting ... for anyone out there, in the now, to claim her shadow-self.

After much shouting, a red flannel blindfold was placed over her eyes, and someone led her off the auction block. Cindy's hands were in front of her. She reached out, making clinking sounds with her chains, random metallic tunes to ward off whatever evil might await her. Cindy wound up in the back of a pickup truck. The feel of the heavy metal truck chugging down the road beneath her was familiar. Curled up in the back of the open truck, she murmured harmonies to the sound of the engine, as the truck bounced along a dirt road. Cindy could smell space. Time moves differently when you can't see. She could feel the sun slowly drying out her wet jeans. She welcomed the warmth on her face. In this unknown world, it calmed her to sing, to hum.

Eventually the truck stopped, and dust billowed all around. She was lifted out of the truck and cradled like a sleeping child. Her blindfold was removed. Bright light diffused the air. As her eyes adjusted, Cindy found herself in a white room. Holes had been cut into each wall for windows, as well as a larger hole for a door. There was a turquoise mat lying on a dirt floor, as if a part of the sky had been placed there for her to rest.

Like a piece of discarded paper, she crumpled onto the mat. Words came from her captor's mouth, something sounding like French but not. He knelt down and began to remove the irons from her swollen ankles. Her ankles were red and bloody, yet Cindy felt no pain. Cindy could see their rawness, yet there was no sensation. Her captor threw the metal shackles and chains outside the door. Gently, like a lover unsure of himself, he reached down and held both of her hands. Unafraid, Cindy stared into his indigo eyes. He helped her up and stood before her, softly singing songs without words. He slowly undid the metal rings holding her wrists together. The sounds of the chains melded with his melody. Cindy stared down at her freed hands. When she looked up, he was gone.

* * *

IN THIS PLACE, there was no need for shackles, as there was no place to go. Even if there was, why would she go? There was no need to seek. CindySleigh had no desire to move. The empty room mimicked the white inner room of her mind, where her thoughts and memory used to clutter, clamoring to be heard like an overfilled library. She looked out over a landscape filled with heaving hills of beige sand.

Cindy sat down cross-legged on the dirt floor and watched the sun pass over the neutral landscape. The shadows, full of lavenders and blues, cut through the blank expanse of sand, making shapes ever changing. Helios' chariot ran its way across the sky, leading the day into dusk.

CindySleigh rubbed her red, inflamed wrists and unconsciously began rubbing her hands together, turning them over and over like Lady Macbeth. "What to do? What to do?" she repeated. There was nothing to do, nowhere to go, no thoughts left. She sat still. She had empty rooms, inside and outside. Cindy was alone, surrounded by a barren land, wringing her hands as though they had been stained with blood that was not hers. "What's done cannot be undone," she mused.

CindySleigh looked down at the dirt floor in front of her. Pieces of pain were scattered about in the form of a broken mirror. Cindy could see only parts of her reflection. The triangular, trapezoidal, and rectangular pieces showed many faces broken. Cindy leaned down close to one of the splintered slivers of silver-coated glass. "My eye is gray." She pulled herself up and away. "My hundred eyes are gray."

Cindy picked up a chunk of glass. She saw her hair chopped short and bright silver. "I am old!" she exclaimed. Cindy noticed dark red rivulets running down her arm, like veins placed on the outside of her skin. "How is it that I do not feel pain?" Part of her multifaceted reflection had sliced her left hand as she searched for a memory in the shards of the looking glass.

Cindy ripped part of her white shirt off at the waist using her teeth. She wound it around her left palm. It was the place Lady Macbeth had washed the stain that would never disappear. Cindy held her hands as if in prayer to apply the necessary pressure to stop the brown-red blood. "Well, at least here's proof. I now know I am real. There's a reflection. There's blood. I actually exist." It was hard to know for sure. The blankness within and the endless beige dunes without seemed more like places that belonged to a specter than a human being.

CindySleigh pressed her hands together hard. She stared up at the heavens. The heavy, bruised, violet-blue clouds billowed up and moved with great speed. Then it began to rain.

It rained. It hailed. Lightning struck all over the desert. It struck near the small white box where Cindy slept. The thunder roared, but she did not hear it. Winds blew through the window holes, but she did not feel them. She remained motionless on her back, while the turbulent weather tried to wake her.

* * *

THE STORM ENDED. Cindy sat up and looked out the door to her new world, seeing a vast and empty horizon. Beige sand, blue sky, and the white sun poured in through the windows and door. Cindy sat on her mat and watched the shadows change as the sun moved from one side of the hemisphere to the other. She had arrived at a place of no destination, a place with no guideposts. Every day, she would walk out and climb the great dunes, wandering aimlessly. It was day and then it was night. Over time, the land became her friend. The sky became her painting. The dried remains of plant or animal life, the fossils of the once living, these took on life for CindySleigh.

Time collapses in on itself, when it is not filled with the constant details of living. CindySleigh seemed to have escaped to where time is simply day or night, without hours, minutes, or seconds to mark its passage. During the day she wandered, during the night she slept. Her story is no story, for, as we know, nothing ever really happens to CindySleigh. She slips away like a small breeze, unnoticed and unobserved.

ON ONE OF these many soothing nondescript days, Cindy noticed a change in the sand on her horizon line. The sand was not moving in the usual way, it was shooting up irregularly like an electrocardiogram of a heart attack. Curious, she walked closer to the spurting sand. She saw a horse, a bleached-white horse. Cindy kept her distance, unsure of this wild creature.

The mare's nostrils flared as she stomped a hoof into the loose sand, moving the grains about. She shook her mane, its bleached strands moved like liquid lightning on either side of her long head. Lifting her eyes to the sky, she stared at the round white disc of the sun, so bright it made the sky chalk white. The mare's body was so scorched that it no longer had color. She tried to shake off the afternoon heat. Beads of sweat went flying into the sand, sizzling, then evaporating as they hit.

The mare closed her eyes, feeling the heat blurring the contours of her own surface with the sky and sand. She snorted and stomped, swished her tail in dismay, reared up, and neighed as if to announce her rage at the day — at *all* days. Then she began to gallop. She ran, hooves sinking in the sand, making her way up and down the hills. Waves of heat vibrated all around her. Her body kept shifting, fading in and out, and still she ran. There was no destination, no hope. Only the constant, enduring pounding of hooves sliding down the dunes only to bound up yet another hill to nowhere.

Cindy watched the horse from a distance. A purple shadow extended from each of its four hooves creating an exaggerated version of the horse's elegant shape as it lunged forward, again and again, into the bright white landscape. The beast randomly flailed about without purpose or path. Cindy stood very still, calling out, silently, to the white-on-white creature. Cindy extended her arms forward and willed with all her heart, "Come to me."

The mare turned her head, shaking her mane, alternately flashing two piercing eyes — one black, one blue, the swords of her state of mind. Cindy returned the horse's stare with unblinking diffused-gray eyes. She kept her arms stretched out before her, for what seemed like eternity, silently commanding the horse to come. An invisible tunnel ran between them, for though they were separate, they were truly one.

The bleached mare heard the silent call of CindySleigh. She tried to shake off the human's stare. She reared up again, letting her voice and body express her rage. Ghostly lines surrounded her, blurring the mare's contours with waves of heat. She whinnied and snorted in response to this human's loving command. When her hooves hit the ground, the mare found herself galloping at full speed towards Cindy's open arms. The sand under the horse shifted as if to propel her. Then a sea of sand split open to make the horse's way clear.

Cindy began to panic. This horse was headed straight for her. She was sure this beast from hell was going to run her down and just keep on going, but still she did not move from where she stood. She kept her arms extended as if for an embrace. Time moved. The sun, low on the horizon, created a brilliant fuchsia-orange light across the dunes.

The shadows became deep as night. Cindy broke into a sweat. The uppermost arc of the sun disappeared below the horizon and the lapis lazuli of twilight appeared. It was the time when all whites turn different shades, bluer than blue. The stars began to make their appearance known — even though they might shine just as brightly during the day — repeating what we see and don't see but is always there. All this in the few seconds of a bounding horse and a woman standing frozen in her spot, hands apart, shaking slightly, wondering the where, how, and why of it all.

The bleached mare stopped suddenly in front of CindySleigh, bowing her head down between Cindy's arms. The sand billowed around them, encircling them with little light-blue clouds. The pair were a little less solid, a little less real. Cindy tilted her head back and forth slowly so she could see into each eye of the horse. First the pale blue eye dragged Cindy into the confusion of the past, the aimless darting, movement without direction. Then Cindy tilted her head the other way to see the other eye, black as a moonless night. She was pulled into a space much like a vortex and transported into another world she could feel but could not see. The black eye was a vacuum pulling her into the unknown.

The bleached mare stomped her front hooves, and Cindy stomped her feet in return. The mare shook her mane and snorted; Cindy shook her silver head of hair and laughed. The dust died down, and they were left with the night, the stars, and each other. CindySleigh walked over and very gently patted the horse's back. A shiver ran down both their spines. Using her hands, Cindy began to methodically brush the bleached horse. She brushed the mane from its eyes, she brushed the sweat from its brow, and she brushed the sand from its coat. Cindy plaited its tail into a braid as one might the hair of a child — a four-legged one that towers over you but remains, with all its emotions, raw and innocent. Cindy looked into the blue eye of the bleached horse and revisited her past with bewilderment. Then she switched to the black eye, and was lead to a place of solace and peace. "Thank you for coming to me," Cindy spoke out loud, for CindySleigh had been missing her emotions in the desert for a very long time.

* * *

THE DAYS OF sky and sand were endless. Without memory, Cindy had no regrets. She focused on the ever-shifting air around her and the taste of sand in her mouth.

As she turned to slide down a dune, a shape to her left caught her eye. She stopped to investigate, and slowly made her way to the shape. Cindy had not seen anything different than the seamless sand and sky for so long, her heartbeat accelerated and a smile spread across her face. She came closer and saw that the contour was sleek and smooth. Breathless, she stood over a dead wolf.

The wolf had been dead for quite a while; Cindy could see Pandora's insects had devoured the wolf's flesh for their own sustenance long ago. Clean white bones and silver fur remained. The wolf appeared to be resting on its left side, seemingly asleep. Its silver fur shimmered in the ever-present sun. Cindy bent down and stroked the wolf's pelt with kindness and respect. "I hope your animal life was a good one," she said out loud.

When she ran her hand along the fur in the wrong direction, it prickled her palm. It was strange how intact the wolf's fur was: a perfect pelt. Cindy lifted it gently off of the bones and laid it aside. "I will use your outside to keep my inside warm on the cold nights. Is that alright with you?"

The bones were silent and unchanging.

Cindy bowed to the essence of the wolf. She left his skeleton above the ground so the sun could warm his bones and his spirit could be free.

The sun moved quickly west, and Cindy carefully folded the fur over her left arm and bowed, one more time, to honor the wolf, before she walked away. Many hours passed until she arrived back in her white room with the blue mat. She smoothed down the wolf pelt over her rectangle of blue as night came upon the desert.

CINDY SLEPT UNDER her silver wolf pelt. This was the season when the days shortened and the nights grew longer and colder. The pelt was warm enough to keep her through the winter. She would stroke the lovely silver fur as she stared out at the stars. The fur would shine elegantly, even in the darkest night. Cindy felt protected by the wolf.

As she slept, Cindy would run with four legs in her dreams. She would swim through streams and shake the droplets of water off her fur. The Silver Wolf was an outsider and was looked upon with disdain. The parameters of place and behavior were not flexible; the Silver Wolf was. Without provocation the Silver Wolf would wrestle other wolves in her pack. Growling, pouncing, she would try to get them to play. The Silver Wolf would leap up in the air for no reason other than for the joy of leaping. The Black Wolf always drew the Silver Wolf in with his teasing shoves and hearty growl. Cindy knew this black wolf, with his navy eyes, well. She would jump on him with all her might, and they would roll on the ground, pushing and biting. He wanted to rein her in, keep her in her place within the pack, but the Silver Wolf would never comply.

The dance with the Black Wolf lasted through the night, while Cindy slept. When she awoke, her hair was all askew. She had scratches on her arms and legs: two bites on her left arm, and one bite on her left leg. In the light of day, she knew the Black Wolf was a powerful, kindred spirit.

The next night, CindySleigh lit her fire at twilight. She managed to loop twine through the eyes of the wolf pelt and attach it to her back. Then she began to dance. As the fire of sunset and the bonfire in the desert grew, she twirled around, swinging the pelt. She jumped up and down with both feet, then quickly turned, playing with the spirit of the wolf. Cindy sang what she believed to be the Silver Wolf's song; it was a combination of a growling howl, high and bright, followed by whimpering. She danced dragging one leg, only to leap about showing the folly of the false lame portion of her dance. Sirius rose high up in the sky, so she did not feel alone as she writhed, jumped, and pretended to be the wolf she was inside. She felt the Black Wolf watching her from the shadows — circling just beyond the light.

Finally, from a lack of oxygen, Cindy stopped behind the fire and looked into the desert, hearing the sand as it shifted in the wind. She felt the breeze drying the sweat off of her face as she untied the pelt from her body and sat facing it on the ground. She found some sticks and created a sawhorse for the wolf pelt. Cindy sat up and stared into the holes that were the Silver Wolf's eyes. "I know you have much to teach me," she murmured. "I will listen. I know how to sit and wait and listen." Then, in the light of the flames, she sat motionless by the skin of the wolf.

CindySleigh felt a nudge from a wet nose and looked up to see the Black Wolf, with its mouth open, tongue out, in a smiling kind of way. She moved forward to touch him, but he backed away. Cindy saw that her arm was covered in silver fur. She ran her hands across her face through hair that now seemed to begin at her chin. Her ears also had a silky touch. When she placed her hands on the sand, they were paws — hands no more. Her thoughts jumped and so did her body, leaping around the fire on all fours instead of on twos. The dark one chased her out into the desert. He was hard to see in the dark. Cindy lifted her nose in the wind; ah, he was to the left of her. She feigned right, and then pounced on him immediately. Their laughter growled way into the night as they dodged and ran while Sirius crossed the sky.

CINDYSLEIGH AWOKE BY her saw-horse wolf and wondered about the shadow worlds where we all might be wolves running and leaping in spirited packs through the darkness. She wondered if she would ever play with the Black Wolf again. These were moments without history or duration, brief interludes of hope, like catching a firefly and releasing it, watching it light the twilight as if by magic.

The desert was an extraordinary place. She patiently waited for whatever might appear along her path. Cindy named the horse Magnificat. The horse was there to brush and love. Cindy could never bring herself to ride Magnificat, for wildness was in its heart, and she wanted the horse to remain completely free. She lay on her piece of sky and fell asleep. She dreamt of being under the earth, of moving her pressed palms up like a seed looking for the light of day. Her digits spread and moved up out of the sand, mimicking winter trees.

* * *

SHE AWOKE TO find dead trees outside her doorway. They were birch trees, white with dark gray striations binding the trunk and limbs. She could hear the trees trembling as the wind whistled a low tune. Occasionally, broken limbs would fall to the ground. She leaned forward to pick them up. They were like bones: an arm bent and curved at the elbow, a hand with a few digits cut off or lost.

Cindy created a pile out of the sticks in front of her doorway. The sky was the orange before the red before the violet before the blue that became night. Her wood was like tangled hair, yet it seemed to have the rhythmic sense of a pile of lines. The key to her creating fire would be where other keys are hidden. Underneath one of the nearby rocks, she found the sulfur sticks to light.

The dry limbs began to glow as the fire fed upon branches of life, long dead. The flames quickly spread, tossing up fireballs, miniature suns, into the sky, as if the fire believed that if it reached high enough, it could touch that eternal space. Cindy heard the trees shivering.

She looked up. Dead leaves hung from all the trees, trembling as if chilled by the brisk wind. Their tips, translucent and curled, reflected the orange of the fire.

The scratching of the ghostlike leaves vibrated above the crack and snap of fire. The sky was changing from red to violet. Cindy tried to count the leaves to quiet her mind, puzzled by their sudden appearance. "How do dead leaves appear by the hundreds on bare branches?" she wondered.

Then they flew. All at once orange-tipped butterflies took off, drifting in patterns that seemed like chaos. They swirled around the fire making an inner-lit tornado. Just as quickly, they disappeared into the dark purple of dusk. Cindy focused on the flames, once bright and high, now burning red and gray. The limbs, crumbling slowly, became ash. She sat and waited for the lapis lazuli of twilight. She sat until the moonless sky let out its stars to glitter above her.

"How did I ever get chained into this body?" Cindy asked the silence. Like the dead-leaf butterflies, Cindy wanted to fly off the branch of a wintering tree, the naked tree that has pulled all of its energy into the earth to await the return of Persephone. Even in the bleakest of times, there is supposed to be promise, there is supposed to be hope. Perhaps that is why people created the idea of life after death. Their own eventual decay and demise carry no whisper of promise. Without memory, there was no desire. No sense of what was missing, or a goal that must be met, or a chore that had to be done, or a person that needed to be tended to. The garden that was her life had totally disappeared, yet living without memory felt like hope. There was only the future. And in the future there was promise. CindySleigh would search for her heart, even though she could not remember how it got ripped out of her chest. She knew it was out there. Somewhere.

* * *

THE NEXT MORNING, Cindy sensed something was different. CindySleigh feared change. Then she realized that the sun was not rising. Cindy kept looking east, earnestly searching the horizon for the one thing she could count on every day in the desert: the sun. For a moment, it was rising. Then it was gone. She could see a brief afterglow in its shape, but the sun did not rise. She was determined to wait it out, force it to rise as it should, so all could see and grow. "The sun has to rise," Cindy told herself over and over again. After many days, if that is what they are called without sunrises, the sun finally arose but shed no light. "What kind of torture is this?" Cindy shouted to the sky. The orb rose and set, but there was no light of day.

Even though it was daytime, it never was bright. Just as the giant orb would rise above the horizon line, its light would disappear. At first, Cindy thought she was going blind as she crept around in darkness. She would mark the days with charcoal from the remains of her fire as the orb came up. Cindy was so sure light would come each day. As she woke up, she sat on her blue mat and scoured the horizon for light. Time was filled with daily tasks, but the sun refused to shine. Her brain gave her no answer. Her heart said there was no sun.

Cindy cried. She sat, then stood, then lay down and slept for as long as she could, for day had become an eternal night. Cindy had to relearn her desert without light. No longer were there shadows by the dunes that she would watch with delight. No longer was the passage of seconds countable by following the sun from one side of the landscape to the other. Disoriented, she slept.

During the endless day-night Cindy tossed about on her piece of sky. In her dreams, she tumbled down through the air, having moved over an edge. With sky under her, above her, all around her, she fell. The wind whistled through her body. She passed through clouds, a montage of white and gray. Time moved like motor-run snapshots, with every second overlayed one on top of the other. Then she felt gravity pulling her, and she moved over another edge. She drooled upward as she fell, too fast to decide anything. All night, she moved over an edge and fell down-up.

The wind blew Cindy outside of her white room, lifting her, then letting her go. Small tornadoes of sand began to swirl violently. The many spirals would reach up, higher and higher, until the sky was no longer visible. Cindy was inside the whistling white sand. All was falling up or flying down. She wasn't sure whether she was asleep or awake.

CindySleigh remained suspended midair, mounting an invisible Jacob's Ladder that floated between desert and sky. All thoughts fell away from her brain, words were scattered and carried away in pieces by the wind and sand. There was only movement. CindySleigh sensed for a time the knowing of not knowing.

WITH A SUDDEN inhalation, Cindy jumped up from her piece of blue sky more awake than she had ever been. The sun appeared on the horizon line, casting all the pastels that delight the senses. First, the lavender, then the blushing pink, turning into a fleshy peach and the light yellow of butter, and finally the white ball of fire leapt up from the horizon and blazed through the sky. The great sun of the desert baked CindySleigh each day. The white of her white clothes were bleached even whiter. Her skin seemed to naturally reject the bronze the sun would have given most beings. She was becoming translucent, and her veins were easily seen pumping blood beneath her opalescent surface. She glowed with all the colors inside a seashell — shimmering blue, lavender, pale yellow, coral, and pale rose — as she mimicked the sunrise and became the land.

The sun was moving in and out of odd-shaped clouds. The sun shone through them like the moon at night. Shadows appeared and disappeared as she walked through the sand. She was so very grateful for the empty-full.

Cindy walked away from her white room and the piece of blue-sky cloth she slept on. She walked straight ahead, not looking back at the remains of the fire and chains from which she had broken free. The big white horse, Magnificat, followed her, matching her pace but always a ways behind her so as not to touch the waves of Cindy's movement. Cindy's body, under what was left of her white garb, moved with ease. She climbed over many dunes. The sand blew through her as she danced in the desert. Her walk had a rhythm that was not rhythmic. Her movements were awkwardly beautiful. The wind picked up, and she reveled in its fierceness. The sand and sky became one.

Cindy could only be seen by the glow of her iridescence. One minute lavender, then flashing gold as the wind pushed through her. Sand sifted through her pores and still she danced forward, the dance in between life and death, air and earth, movement and stillness. "It's all here, all the time." There was no sense to sense. Cindy's movements became very fluid, but she did not move forward anymore.

Magnificat stopped and stared at Cindy. The mare stared with her blue eye, the eye of the present, seeing only the future of each passing moment. Then the mare reared up on her hind legs and neighed. With a high-pitched snort, she demanded the presence of CindySleigh, for the horse could make out Cindy no more. Only a glistening golden figure appeared, in the far distance, gliding over the crest of of a dune.

CINDY WAS LOOKING out at a vast sea. She broke out into a sprint, stopping just in front of the water. Cindy looked out upon the horizon. She glanced down at her two feet planted on the earth. Cindy lifted her right foot and stepped into the water. The moment she touched the water, CindySleigh exploded into flames, all the elements completing her: Earth, Air, Water, and the spark of Fire we call Life. As the four elements came together, Cindy fell back into the black that followed.

* * *

IN SOME NO-TIME Cindy filled her collapsing lungs with a deep, fast inhale and found herself shackled in the rain, soaked through, standing on the slave-auction block, listening to the sounds of the auctioneer. "What will you pay for this?" Cindy suddenly jerked her head up straight as she heard a voice she recognized. Father Michael stood firm, and Cindy saw the wild dog at his side, nuzzling and biting his hand.

"I'd bid my heart for this woman, but I cannot for it is forever bound to her. I will pay whatever you ask, for money is but a dream, and so is CindySleigh," Father Michael said.

The auctioneer was stunned. The priest's words cast mirrors in front of the auctioneer and all the buyers. They could no longer see CindySleigh, only themselves.

The auctioneer mouthed the words, "Just take her," watching his own reflection, in shock.

Father Michael helped Cindy off of the block, took the key from the stunned keeper, and unlocked her manacles. He put his robe around her and swiftly spirited her away, with the wild dog, Black, nipping at their heels.

the death of a butterfly

www.ingramcontent.com/pod-product-compliance
Lightning Source LLC
Chambersburg PA
CBHW050758250626
47155CB00005B/2120